the
DARK
backward

FORTHCOMING BY JULIA BUCKLEY

Pity Him Afterwards:
A Madeline Mann Mystery

West Vancouver
Memorial Library

In memory of
Marilyn D. Jones

the DARK backward

Julia Buckley

MIDNIGHT INK
WOODBURY, MINNESOTA

First Edition
First Printing, 2006

Book design by Donna Burch
Cover design by Kevin R. Brown
Author photo by Kristina Sado, 2005 (www.sadofoto.com)

Midnight Ink, an imprint of Llewellyn Publications

Library of Congress Cataloging-in-Publication Data
Buckley, Julia, 1964–
    The dark backward / Julia Buckley. — 1st ed.
        p. cm.
    ISBN-13: 978-0-7387-0826-3
    ISBN-10: 0-7387-0826-7
    1. Policewomen—Fiction. 2. Women private investigators—Fiction. 3. Rape victims—Fiction. 4. Governors—Fiction. 5. Family secrets—Fiction. 6. Murder—Investigation—Fiction. I. Title.

PS3602.U2648D37 2006
813'.6—dc22
                                      2006042026

Midnight Ink
Llewellyn Publications
2143 Wooddale Drive, Dept. 0-7387-0826-7
Woodbury, MN 55125-2989, U.S.A.
www.midnightinkbooks.com

Printed in the United States of America

To the Buckley boys
Jeff, Ian, and Graham

and

To my parents,
Katherine Ebbes Rohaly
and
William Rohaly

"Then live, Macduff: what need I fear of thee?
But yet I'll make assurance double sure,
And take a bond of fate: thou shalt not live;
That I may tell pale-hearted fear it lies,
And sleep in spite of thunder."

Macbeth, Act IV, Scene I

"What seest thou else
In the dark backward and abysm of time?"

The Tempest, Act I, Scene II

"When the president does it, that means it's not illegal."

Richard M. Nixon

PROLOGUE

WHEN LILY CALDWELL DIED, it didn't feel the way it was described by people who had those "life after life" experiences. She didn't float above herself, watching her body on the table as the doctor's desperate fingers tried to stanch the blood that filled her lung, torn by a bullet. She didn't walk down a tunnel in pursuit of an elusive yet beckoning light, nor did she see a man with a benign face holding out a hand, offering to reunite her with her late father. What Lily saw, very clearly, was the face of her murderer—and the act—in slow motion.

She saw herself crouched behind her squad car, shouting hoarsely for backup into the radio in her hand. "Officer down," she'd said, holding back the tears for Danny Donovan, her partner, who was almost assuredly dead. In death, she saw the enemy approach her, the gun in his hand, confident in the knowledge that she didn't sense his presence, saw him lift the weapon, saw him pull the trigger just as she turned to receive the impact full in the chest, her arms flying outward as if to embrace eternity, her head landing in a puddle left by the recent rain.

In death, Lily saw the truth that the afterlife had given her: the man's face. It was illuminated, as it hadn't been in the darkness of that rain-cleansed night, ablaze with revelation. That the face belonged to the most powerful man in the state did not daunt Lily one bit, at least not until the doctor said, "There, goddammit!" and managed to dam the river of her blood. "We have a pulse, Doctor!" cried a nurse, and with a wail of anguish Lily came back to the pain: the pain of a bitter wound, the pain of the loss of her partner, and the pain caused by the extinguishing of that light, that clear and irrefutable light that had shown her, in the seven and a half minutes that she had been dead, that Governor Robert "Nob" Stevens was her murderer.

Of course, no one believed her. Lily had always been stubborn, and their incredulity didn't faze her much. She had no evidence, so she didn't hold it against the officers of the law—her comrades—that they wouldn't take her part in pursuing the course of justice. It fell on her, she knew, to find the proof she needed, and she was willing to do whatever it took.

For that reason, ultimately, she was fired. She'd been sent to the department shrink; she'd been counseled by the department minister; she'd had many a heart-to-heart with her chief, who had been one of Danny's best friends. Lily was loved, and all of her colleagues were glad she was alive, but no one wanted to work with her, not when she insisted on clinging to the ridiculous notion that the governor had killed her partner and shot a hole in her chest with a semiautomatic pistol. She'd been counseled to let it go, advised to let it go, and then ordered to let it go.

She didn't let it go.

She held no grudge against Chief Paluzzi for firing her. She understood his feelings, and in his place she knew she would feel the same; she'd always been a practical woman. Death had been a gift, though.

That was what Lily ultimately believed, and she had to be true to the vision that continued to haunt her each night when she closed her eyes.

She blamed no one for her current isolation and blamed no one for her firing, but she did blame one man for not believing her. Maybe Paluzzi couldn't wrap his mind around her seven and a half minutes of truth, but one man should have taken her word against all odds. That man was Grayson Caldwell, her soon-to-be ex-husband.

Lily, thirty years old, jobless, and thought by many to be shell-shocked into worthlessness, intended to continue her crusade. She was armed only with the knowledge that death by shooting had brought her and with the name of a girl she didn't know, a teacher who'd been dead for seventeen years: Emily Martin.

ONE

Lily barely managed to hide her distaste for the man who sat across from her in the diner. He had hired her, and he was entitled to her time as long as she was billing him, but she didn't have to like him in the privacy of her own heart. He was the "Am I right or am I right?" type, and she understood why his wife was having an affair even as he talked at her with his mouth full, his eyes occasionally dropping to observe her breasts, his hands busy sawing his steak with surprising precision.

"So she met with him both times?" he asked her, wiping steak sauce from his lip with a fat forefinger.

"Yes, Mr. Grant. She went to the Seasons Motel, Room 47, and stayed each time for about two hours. I have photos of her entering and leaving the room. As I told you, I don't peep at windows."

"But the guy went into the room, too?"

"You have the photos," she said, pushing them toward him with growing impatience. She had work to do, and she wanted to be off of his clock so that she could punch in on her own.

"So what do I do now?" he asked, surprising her.

"What . . ." Lily fought the urge to laugh. "Well, sir, I would talk things over with my wife."

He shook his head, grinning. His face looked ugly with ill intention. "Talk things over?"

Lily didn't like intimidators. "Obviously there are things the two of you need to work out. If you can work it out, do it. If you can't, get a divorce. I'm just the investigator." She slid to the end of her booth, indicating her willingness to be finished with the meeting.

"So what do I owe you?" he asked, choosing to be amused.

"This is a week of work at three hours per night. I've put a copy of the bill in your folder, but I told you my rates up front. You owe me twenty-one hundred dollars." Lily met his glance without flinching, and he nodded.

"You're a tough little lady," he said. "And pretty. I'm surprised a cute thing like you is in a business like this. I always liked brunettes. That dark-haired, gypsy look." He was assessing Lily as though for a photo shoot.

"Right," Lily responded, forcing a smile. "I assume you'll send a check promptly?"

"Or what? You get goons to beat me up?"

"I'll beat you up myself, and cut out the middleman," she answered, making it a joke. People didn't believe that Lily, who was only five foot three and rather thin, could do any damage, and she liked it that way. It gave her the element of surprise. Only the men and women at the police academy, who had trained with her and had seen her in action on the mat, knew what sort of power was housed in Lily's small body.

Grant laughed. "I like you," he said. "I think I just might find some more work for you in the future. Unless you want to go on my payroll? I'm sure I could find a job for you at the factory."

She didn't bother to hide her shudder. "No thanks. I like sunlight."

5

Grant laughed once more and tossed two twenties on the table so that he could escort her out. In the parking lot he thanked her again and offered to see her to her car.

"That won't be necessary. Good luck, Mr. Grant," she said. She waited until he drove away, then hurried out of the lot, bound for home. It was autumn, and she had decided to walk the six blocks to the diner. She hadn't been indulging enough in the wood-smoke-scented air of fall, her nose buried as it was in books or online searches, and she knew she needed exercise to keep her strength up. Between work and her full-time hobby, she hadn't been enjoying much of a life.

She sighed as she contemplated this, and somehow an image of Gray entered her head—Gray as he had been when their marriage was happy. Before she could gird herself against the pain, it was there, clutching her middle, making it hard to breathe, stabbing fiercely into the most vulnerable part of her, the part she couldn't defend with her hands. She stopped walking and leaned over, her palms on her knees, looking like a winded runner and puffing out breaths in the same manner.

"Lily," someone called, and she stood up and spun around just in time to sense that he intended to harm her. His burly body leaned forward, and his hands were out, reaching. Danny's voice was ever in her mind in these situations: *Never let someone's size intimidate you, Lil. You're a weapon. You have skill.*

Instinctively she threw her purse aside and prepared to fight. Her assailant was surprised in mid-lunge; he'd obviously expected her to run, which had never been Lily's way. Gray had told her that she must have an interesting brain chemistry, since women were wired for flight due to the oxytocin released by their brains after the initial adrenaline rush. Lily suggested that she had more testosterone than the average woman, and Gray had laughingly agreed.

Now she darted nimbly aside from the mugger's rugby-type thrust and came up with a swift knee in his groin; he grunted but didn't go down, and Lily's fist met his nose in a straight punch, in perfect academy form.

"Aaahg!" he cried, his eyes surprised and almost afraid. He hadn't expected her to fight, and the words "didn't sign on for this" went through her mind as she flashed out her foot in a final, quelling kick aimed right between his legs and into the soft flesh of his testicles.

He grunted, landed on his knees, and then slumped to his side like a felled sequoia. He was big, light-skinned, fairly young, and clean shaven.

A woman stepped out on her porch. Lily's ears were still loud with her own rushing blood. "I saw that," the woman shouted, in a voice like a distant bell. "Do you need help?"

"Call the police," Lily answered.

"You sure you're okay, Lily?" asked Marvin Edwards, the driver of the squad car that had picked up her mugger.

"Yeah. I'd still like to walk home, walk him out of my system," she said.

"I don't know . . . ," Marvin began, but he saw Lily's face and held up his hands in mock defense. "Okay, okay. I don't want you to do that to me. Man. Right in the balls."

Marvin winced empathetically, then patted her arm. "You come when you can for the paperwork."

Lily nodded, forced a smile, and waved as Marvin turned off his Mars light and pulled away from the curb. She had calmed considerably since the police car had arrived; her main fear had been that the man would recover and make a run for it, but she'd done enough damage that he'd remained on the sidewalk, unmoving, trying not to add to the pain that coursed through him. Her other fears had been repressed and would be dealt with later, if at all. Lily didn't have much patience for women who indulged their terrors, and it was only in nightmares that she couldn't control her own.

She began to walk again on slightly rubbery legs, and it was then that it dawned on her: *the mugger had called her Lily*.

Governor Nob Stevens was a busy man. At no point in his career had he felt there were enough hours in the day; therefore, he noted the surprise on his secretary's face when he told her he'd take the call from John Pierre on his private line and that she should tell the man in the lobby to wait. "Tell Senator Schwartz I'll be right with him," he said, despite the fact that he'd kept the man waiting for nearly an hour already.

She left the room, her face a blank mask. He'd chosen her out of the mass of clerks in the office when he'd realized that she was non-judgmental; if she did censure him or his daily delegations, she repressed it well, and that was all he cared about. He needed to be surrounded by people who understood the power of his authority. For the same reason, he'd liked John Pierre, who had initially been a bodyguard until Stevens had sensed both his intelligence and his admiration. Pierre had quickly moved up through the ranks until he was personal assistant to the governor, a role with a diverse job description, much of which could never be acknowledged in writing.

The governor snatched the phone. "Stevens," he barked.

"Sir, you asked for an update—"

"So?"

"Ms. Caldwell is, as you suspected, still pursuing the idea that you shot her. The doctors I interviewed assured me that this type of erroneous conclusion is an understandable result of, uh, tragic circumstances and that her obsession is a natural psychological response to trauma."

"You didn't mention specific—"

"Of course not, sir." Pierre's voice was mildly insulted.

"It's bad enough that the rumor was floating around the police station, although at least I was notified. We need to keep an eye on this little crusade. I have a campaign to run, for God's sake."

"Yes, sir."

"The husband still out of the picture?"

"Yes, sir. She's filed for divorce."

"So she's on her own. What's she been looking for?"

"Our monitoring of her computer reveals that she is looking for anything connected to the name Emily Martin or to Nazareth High School, where this Miss Martin had been a teacher. She's also been at the library, hunting through public records. And she's been looking into . . . you. Your schedules, your tour dates, your public functions. She's tried to find out about some private things, too—even what you do on holidays. She's been a very busy girl."

Stevens's grip on the phone tightened. He caught a glimpse of himself in the mirror that he kept next to his office door. At fifty-nine, he was still a handsome man, he thought. He had a full head of silver hair, a pleasant and trustworthy face, and a physique kept trim by regular workouts and occasional liposuction. He noted now that his whole body had tensed, hardened, and his face had aged in the five minutes since he had last glanced at himself. He wouldn't have this getting out of control; he wouldn't allow this little pipsqueak ex-cop to ruin his life, his looks, even his day.

He took a deep breath, opened his drawer, and took out a butter-scotch candy. He unwrapped it with great deliberation, humming tunelessly while he thought about Pierre's information.

"What about our warning?" he asked.

9

There was a pause. "That didn't go well," Pierre said.

"What?"

"Our ambassador misunderstood his role. He ended up looking like a mugger. She took him down, called the police."

"For Christ's sake," Stevens hissed, almost choking on his butterscotch. "He's in custody?"

"Yes, sir."

"Did he say anything to her? Tell her to back off?"

"All he said was her name, sir."

"Son of a bitch. I expect better from you, Pierre. This guy can't connect this to me or you, can I at least believe that?"

"No, he can't, sir. And the message, had it been delivered, wouldn't be understood by anyone but her. He was simply to suggest that she was wrong in her assumptions, maybe to imply that he knew the truth about her assault."

"But instead he tried to assault her."

"He says she misunderstood his intentions."

Stevens swore, picked up a pencil from his blotter, and flung it across his opulent office. "Let's not hire any more idiots, Pierre."

"No, sir."

"This girl, she's a thorn in my side. She's a local hero, a sob story. Pretty cop gets shot, loses partner, crime is never solved. Then this pretty cop gets fired. The press had a field day with that one. Imagine if the pretty cop wanted to come forward with her cock-and-bull story about how she saw the governor's face in the hereafter. That kind of thing could kill a career, untrue as it may be."

"I totally understand, sir." There was real concern in Pierre's voice. Stevens couldn't help it; he liked the kid: his eagerness, his energy, his wonderful gift for sycophancy.

"I'd invite her here to talk with me, but we'll make that a last resort. We can't have it backfiring, have her making some kind of crazy scene. Plus I want her believing that I know nothing about it. That's safer, for now."

"Yes, sir."

"You keep me updated, and make this thing with the mugger go away."

"Yes, I will, sir."

Stevens hung up the phone with a sort of weariness, which was rare for him. He was so busy, and his life was so important, that there was no possibility of being dragged into the past, forced to contemplate things he hadn't thought about in years. What was done was done, and Stevens knew better than anyone that sometimes in life difficult decisions had to be made. Real men—men like him—had the ability and the vision to make them.

He would deal with little Lily Caldwell the way he'd dealt with every other potential threat in his life: he would bulldoze her into the ground. She had no business sniffing around for signs of Emily Martin, no right. Emily belonged to the past—his past—and he'd be damned if some silly woman was going to try to intimidate him.

No one needed to know about Emily, and while he had life left coursing through his very healthy veins, no one ever would.

TWO

LILY'S HOUSE WAS NEAT as a pin, which only emphasized her loneliness. Her husband had been sloppy, endearingly so, and she'd forever been picking up his discarded clothing and neatening the papers left in his wake: file folders, jotted notations and computations, even test tubes that somehow made it home from the lab. Grayson had never understood that he was untidy; if Lily mentioned it, he would focus on her with a bemused expression, as if trying to translate her complaint from another language. It was lucky for them both that she found this amusing and was able to laugh off their "odd couple" existence.

Now the loss of his clutter was a consistent reminder of his absence, and Lily felt it, persistent as a toothache, whenever she entered her house. Because of that she lingered in her front yard, snapping the heads off some hardy marigolds in her autumnal garden, then enjoying the sharp, lovely scent the dying flowers left on her fingers. Gray had designed their little plot, drawing the plan with his scientist's precision and then leaving Lily to buy and plant the seeds and to see to their nurturing. Their life had been that way from the start: a natural partnership in every project, a consistent recognition of each other's talents. They took turns driving the car. Lily paid the bills, but Gray balanced the checkbook. Lily would initiate making love as often as Gray did.

She flicked the dead marigold leaves behind the bushes that fronted her house. She saw a certain symbolism in her flowers. They bloomed, they were beautiful, they basked in the sun, and then they died and were snipped away without further acknowledgment of what they had been. Her love for Gray had seemed eternal. She never questioned its apparent perfection or looked for flaws beneath the surface. When the hurt came, therefore, it was gut-wrenching.

Lily had always been tough. Danny had jokingly referred to her as "brutal" when they'd started out as partners. She'd give a lecture to some youngsters out after curfew, and Danny would chuckle afterward in the car, saying, "You're brutal, Lil. You even scared that big one with the scar on his eye." Sometimes he called her Brutus. Lily, strangely proud of the nickname, had been desperate to impress Danny—twenty years her senior with thirty years on the force—from the very start.

Her tough persona had fallen apart with Danny's death, her hospitalization, her firing, her separation from Gray. Her life began a downward spiral that seemed never to end; her pride in her uniform—and the confidence she wore with it—diminished. The old Lily could have handled one of those tragedies, but all of them together had changed her, emptied her, left her vulnerable in a way that she had always refused to be.

Losing Gray had been the last straw. She wore her toughness still and was ever alert, even paranoid, but inside she had changed, and she hated to admit it. The tears in her eyes as she climbed her porch were the clearest evidence of her weakened self. The old Lily had never cried.

She thought things couldn't get much worse until she walked in her front door and saw Gray sitting on her couch. He rose hesitantly;

the glasses that he wore while he worked were missing, and she had an unrestricted view of his gray eyes—gray like his name, gray like her life.

"Hello, Lily," he said.

Her emotional armor was donned quickly. "Are you here because you signed the papers? You could have given them to my lawyer." She wiped at her eyes and pretended to sort through the mail that she'd picked up on the way in, but she didn't see anything. The letters were cold in her ungloved hands.

"I'm here to apologize." His tone was rueful, and Lily's defenses slipped slightly. She stole a glance at him, but her face remained hard.

"You had months to apologize, Gray. Please don't do this to me today. I'm hating my job, and on top of that I just got mugged."

He seemed to notice her condition for the first time: her messy hair, the jacket her assailant had torn on his descent to the pavement. He rushed to her side. "Are you all right? Did he hurt you?"

She allowed his attention for a moment, overwhelmed by the memories that just the touch of his hand brought to her. "I'm okay. He's under arrest. Marvin and his new partner came and picked him up. I have to go and press—"

"What did he want?" Gray's face had changed from concerned to something else. Normally she was good at discerning nuances of expression, but today she was tired, defeated. She set the pile of letters down on an end table and put her hands on her hips.

"I don't know! Money? Sex? What the hell do any of these guys want, Gray?"

He still looked at her strangely. "Did he take your money? Or try to take it?"

"No. No, I tossed my purse aside, and—"

"Did he go after it?"

14

"No." She was thoughtful now, remembering. "No, that was kind of weird. He never asked for my money, but of course it all happened in seconds. I just reacted."

Gray smiled slightly. "Kicked him?"

"And one good punch in the nose. I didn't break it, but he doesn't know that yet."

"So if he didn't ask for your money, what did he say?"

She rubbed her arms. This was the thought she'd been trying to repress. "He said, 'Lily.' Like he was calling me."

Gray stared. "He wasn't a mugger."

"Of course he was, Gray. A mugger by definition—"

"Doesn't know his victim's name." His face was pale.

Lily shrugged. "I'm not going to talk about this with you. I want some tea, and I want some television. I don't want to think, and I sure don't want to deal with you. No offense," she said bitterly, walking out of the room and into her kitchen. She flipped on the light, opened a cabinet door, and rustled around for a box of tea bags.

Gray had followed her; she felt his presence without having heard his footsteps, and she was suddenly angry. She turned to yell at him, to tell him to get out, but his face stopped her. Normally handsome and full of laughter, dominated by his intelligent, cloudlike eyes and framed by dark, wavy hair, his countenance today was something between grim and fearful, like someone who's just learned he's terminal. Her objection froze in her throat. "What is it?" she asked. He was near enough that she could smell him, the scent of his morning soap and a touch of his citrus aftershave.

He shook his head. "How have you been? I've left messages. You haven't called back. Have you been going to Dr. Alvarez for your follow-ups? Why didn't you call me?"

She pushed past him, grabbing a mug from her dish rack. "You know why I didn't call you. We're not married. It's been a year since the injury. Dr. Alvarez doesn't need to see me anymore."

"Don't be so goddamn defensive, Lily. You know I still love you. You know I don't want the divorce. And I know that what you really want is an apology, and I'm here to give it. That and a warning."

"A warning?" Her lips curled sarcastically as she filled her kettle with water at the tap. "You're so dramatic nowadays, Gray. What happened to that boring scientist I fell in love with?"

She turned her mocking gaze on him and saw not so much anger as a sort of desperate impatience. He took the kettle away, slammed it on the stove, and said, "*Lily*. I apologize. I should never have doubted what you said, and I admit I doubted you. I thought you'd had a dream, a vivid dream, and—"

"I know what you thought." She scowled at him.

"But I was wrong. Okay? I believe you now, and I admit that I shouldn't have doubted you, because you asked me not to, you asked me to believe that it was true."

Her instincts were coming back to her, and she read something on his face. "But that's not the only reason you believe me now when you didn't then. You know something."

He slumped into a chair at her table, and she sat down across from him with a floating sensation, a sense of déjà vu. He met her glance with a searching one of his own. "Lily. You know why I fell in love with you?"

Lily shrugged. "Because you said I looked like Natalie Wood."

He nodded. "Yeah, that's true. That's why I asked you out, that first time I saw you with Danny at the lab, but after that it was because I realized that you were honest. Deeply honest, in a way that I didn't think people really were. And you were unaware of how that distinguished you from the rest of the world. Even when I didn't believe you, I knew that I should, because you wouldn't lie to me or to yourself."

Lily felt her metaphorical chain mail clang to the ground, and without it she felt too exposed. She folded her arms over her chest, giving nothing. She continued to glare at him. "Okay, I'm honest. Are you almost finished, Gray?"

He inched closer, dragging his chair legs across her linoleum. "So even after I hurt you, after you kicked me out, I knew on some level that I had to help you. So I started to look into it, into any reason why the governor would want to have you killed."

"Not *have me* killed. To kill me."

"To kill you," he amended, wincing at his error.

"And you found out I was right? Is that what you're telling me?" Hope surged into her so quickly that she couldn't repress it. She lowered her eyes and toyed with the napkin holder on her table. One sad paper napkin sat inside, dispiritedly folding in on itself.

He took her hand and squeezed it. "What I found was Archie Halsted. Have you ever heard of him?"

Her eyes met his briefly, then flicked away, despite the promise of something she saw there, a hint that her random hunting might finally be rewarded with a clue, something with which she could begin to form a pattern. "No. Should I have heard of him?"

"He worked in the crime lab, back in the late eighties. The police lab, like me. I never met him; I wasn't there then."

"So?" she asked. She pressed too hard on the napkin holder and tipped it over. She reached out to right it, and Gray grabbed her wrist tightly. "Ouch! Gray, what is your problem?"

He stared, then pointed. She looked at the tiny thing on the inside of the napkin holder, something she never would have noticed if he hadn't aimed his finger at it. Instinctively she kept silent as she leaned in for a better look. She had never worked vice and had never done any undercover surveillance, but she was pretty sure she knew a bug when she saw one.

She raised her eyebrows at him, and he said, "Listen, I've got to get going. You're right; I'm being crazy. I just wanted to apologize and to tell you I love you, and . . ." As he said these words, Gray beckoned her up and began to pull her toward the door. "I understand if you still hate me, Lily, but say you'll consider my apology."

"I'll consider it," she said, her eyes searching his. "But I'd like you to leave now."

"Okay. Goodbye, Lily."

"Goodbye, Gray."

When the door closed they were both on the other side of it, and they ran toward Gray's car, which was parked down the street. *That's why I didn't notice it*, Lily thought vaguely as they ran.

"God, I hope there's not a bug in the car. I never thought to look," he said. "And now they'll know about Archie, dammit!"

Once in Grayson's Jeep, she confronted him. "Tell me, Gray, right now! Who is this guy? Why should I care? Who's bugging my house?"

He took her hand in his. "Archie was on duty when the coroner investigated the death of Emily Martin."

Lily's brow furrowed. "But there was no investigation. The coroner ruled it an accident, and there was nothing left to autopsy because of the fiery crash."

"That's what everyone thought. But there was a body, a charred body. The coroner had it on her table that night and was proceeding with an autopsy for a suspicious death, as the investigating officer ordered."

"But the investigating officer was Rich Marcus, and he never ordered—"

"He did, Lily. He did. But someone persuaded him to change his mind. The coroner was told to forget it and that it was no longer being considered suspicious, that the family didn't want an autopsy. The final remains were cremated—more than they'd already been, you might say—and given back to the girl's parents."

"But?"

"But not before the coroner had sent a tissue sample to Archie Halsted. Eventually he was told to destroy it."

"But?"

"But he didn't."

Lily leaned back in the seat, considering the meaning of this. Emily Martin, aged twenty-three, had been killed in 1989 when her car had gone off the road one night on a Capitol City highway. Her story had briefly appeared in the papers, accounts that Lily had read so many times in the past year that she basically knew them by heart. After a week or so, Emily Martin had been forgotten, as had her death by incineration, replaced inevitably by other tragedies, other news.

There had been no official investigation into Emily's death, but apparently that hadn't sat well with Rich Marcus, because at some point the Martin file had been put quietly back into the "Unsolved" file cabinet, maybe just before Marcus retired in '98. In any case, when Chief Paluzzi had ordered everyone on his team to take an unsolved case as a part of their daily workload, Danny had selected Emily Martin. He and Lily had just begun to pursue it after their daily rounds were done, somehow carving out time amidst all of their normal tasks to make some phone calls and try to establish contacts. They'd gotten as far as Nazareth High School and a nun named Sister Jean Baptiste, who was its principal. They had made an appointment to meet with her on a Friday morning, and on that Thursday night they had been coming back from a domestic-disturbance call on the forest preserve road when they saw a car on the shoulder, its flashers blinking red in the darkness. They pulled up behind it and radioed their location.

Danny was making a joke when he stepped out of the cruiser, something about a duck that goes into a bar, and he sent her his humorous look, the one that promised this punch line would elicit a groan. "Hang on," he said. He walked up to the other car, a Cadillac with no license plate, and met his death with Lily looking on, her eyes wide with disbelief and shock as she watched Danny's body arch and crumple. There was no sound before he fell, and she briefly realized, even as she catapulted from the car and ran for cover behind it, that whoever was inside that Caddy had used a silencer.

Danny's murderer—her assailant—had never been caught, but Lily knew his face. She watched it regularly on the television news, and she saw it in nightmares, the ones in which she failed to save Danny over and over again, in which she relived his death in painful punishment for her lack of awareness, her horrible inability to help her partner even as he looked death in the face. She'd sat, waiting to hear about the duck in the bar, and it was only in telling that truth that she'd broken down with the department-appointed counselor. "I'll never know the end of the joke," she cried, as though that were the cause of her constant burden of regret, of the panic attacks, of the nightmares, of the inability to function as an officer of the law.

When she'd finally gone back to work, the Martin file—with all of her notes, her contacts, and the details of Martin's mysterious death—had disappeared.

Now she stared at her husband and tried to make sense of his words. "But what use could a tissue sample be? What would we—"

"If the governor is concerned about Emily Martin, then the governor has something to hide regarding Emily Martin," Gray said, his lips a thin, determined line.

It was the first time he'd acknowledged her theory in words, and relief rushed through her veins like warm water. "How do you know this? How do you know anything about this Archie?"

Gray shrugged. "Like I said, Lily, I've been looking. Maybe it was my penance. I talked to the coroner from that night. Her name was Doctor—"

"Evelyn Striker. I spoke with her, too. She didn't tell me any of this."

"I think her conscience may have been working since she talked to you. Or maybe it's because I'm a fellow scientist; I followed my nose and asked some questions that came to me as hunches. Finally I got the name of Archie and the fact that he'd been sent a sample. Dr. Striker assumed the sample had been destroyed. But I hunted Archie down. It took me weeks to find him, and—"

"He's alive?"

"Yes, alive, and he spoke with me on the phone. He was hesitant—careful—but I told him I was your husband and that I believed you'd been shot because of your investigation of the death of Emily Martin."

"And?"

"And that was yesterday. He hinted that the tissue still existed, and he agreed to meet with me. Today. He's retired now; he has a cabin up in the northwoods. About two hours away." He sat back in his seat and watched her, still clutching her hand and waiting for her response with the hopeful air of a child.

She contemplated Gray, his intense eyes and his repentant face. She hadn't pulled her hand away, and she didn't intend to. She edged ever so slightly closer, and he didn't miss the body language.

"Lily," he said. Two tentative syllables.

She couldn't tear her eyes away. Her protective armor was gone now, and it was just her and Gray for the first time, perhaps, since she had told him to stop nursing her and listen to something she had to tell him. He'd been a wonderful caretaker after the shooting, tender and devoted and gentle. He hadn't been horrified by her ugly wound, only angry that she'd endured it, and she would have considered him the best husband, their marriage the finest and strongest, if she hadn't seen that look in his eyes when she'd told him about Stevens. Gray had made a mistake, such a mistake, when he'd decided to pity her.

She'd warned him long before the shooting, before their marriage even, when she'd been ready to live with him but first determined to tell him about the rape: "You can't feel sorry for me," she'd said. "You can't ever pity me, or it will be over between us."

Gray had known his error instantly, there in their home, where she'd told him the truth about her vision; he had most certainly seen it in her face, because she'd watched him recoil in response to her expression. From that point on things weren't right between them, and a month later Gray had left, at her request. *Six months ago*, Lily reflected, and yet sometimes it felt as though a century had passed.

Now here he was, no different than he'd ever been, no less love in his expression, and no pity. The pity was gone.

"I missed you so much," he said, carrying her hand to his lips and pressing them warmly against her palm. "I love you, Lily. I'm sorry I hurt you."

She wanted to kiss him. She wanted it more than anything at this moment, more even than she wanted to know who'd placed that bug in her kitchen, but Lily was practiced at repressing emotion, and her mind told her it wasn't appropriate to simply take Gray back in without determining that he really believed in her. What if Archie Halsted led nowhere, like all of the leads she'd pursued so far? Would Gray lose this energy, this chivalrous desire to champion her cause? And would the look creep back into his eyes?

22

"I know you are," she said, trying to sound brisk. "I appreciate the apology."

His scent floated to her, and the warmth of his body was like a magnet, drawing her closer. He leaned in.

"No." She pulled her hand away. "I'm sorry. I'm not ready for that."

Gray nodded; his face changed, and he cleared his throat. "Okay. Can we hold off on the divorce, at least?"

"Let's just find Archie Halsted, okay? I need to think about things."

She averted her gaze, but not before she'd gotten one good look into his eyes. It was painful, seeing his hurt, his confusion. Still, she wasn't ready. There was only so much conflict she could handle in one day.

"Let me use your cell phone, Gray," was all she said.

———————

Chief Anthony Paluzzi couldn't believe his ears when he heard Lily's voice. She hadn't spoken to him since the day she'd been fired. He'd tried to call her a few times, but then he'd given up. Lily needed time, he figured, and some therapy, and until then there was no point in looking for her forgiveness.

"Lily?" he said.

"Chief, I need your help. Someone bugged my house. If you don't believe me, you can talk to Gray. He found it." Her voice wasn't defensive, but the words were, and they stung.

"Of course I believe you, Lily. I'll send out some guys to do a sweep. Wait there, and—"

"I'm leaving town for the day. I'm pursuing a lead, and I won't be back until late tonight, I'm guessing. I'll leave my key with my neighbor at number 771, so the guys can use that to get in. The bug we found was in the kitchen napkin holder."

Paluzzi had a bad feeling in his gut. "Lily, where is it that you're going? Is Gray going with you?"

"Yeah, Gray is here right now."

"Good, good. I had heard that you two—"

"You heard right, Chief, but he's here right now." Her tone said *No Trespassing*. Lily was such a blend of toughness and vulnerability that she'd inadvertently found the tiny soft spot in Paluzzi's heart long ago; her most endearing quality was her total unawareness of her own obvious insecurities. Her voice now, sounding so small and yet so brave, brought out his paternal side, the side that he knew Lily hated. "Listen, Lily—"

"I have to go, Chief. I'll be back in touch."

She hung up, and Paluzzi stared at his phone. He had two daughters who somehow didn't make him feel as befuddled and protective as Lily did. He'd called her "hon" once—a slip of the tongue rather than a deliberate condescension—and she'd flared up at him, her large brown eyes brilliant with anger in her small face. Now, hearing the sound of her voice, he remembered the way she'd looked in the hospital, pale and beaten, helpless as a stringed puppet with all the tubes and wires. The first thing she'd said when she'd opened her eyes and seen Paluzzi's face at her bedside was, "Danny's been shot." Lily hadn't been blessed with amnesia as a result of her trauma. She remembered almost everything, and what she didn't remember she said she saw in a "vision" in the time that she'd been dead on the table.

Now Paluzzi wondered if he'd been totally fair to her. What could it have hurt to put out a few feelers and explore her contention? No one would have had to know. Just her and him. Maybe he could still do that for her. Especially if Lily intended to go and get herself shot again. He didn't think he could endure it twice.

He picked up the phone.

Gray pulled away from the curb. Lily had changed her clothes and packed a few snacks into a bag for them, just as she'd always done when they took a road trip. "I brought you a bottle of water," she said as she climbed into the car. She wore jeans and an academy sweatshirt. Gray was impressed anew by her lack of rancor toward the Capitol City police. They'd been her heroes since she was a child, and they remained her heroes today.

"Thanks," he said. They drove for a while in an uneasy silence. There was much that Gray wanted to say but knew she didn't want to hear. If nearly losing Lily to a bullet hadn't made him realize how much he loved her, six months away from her certainly had. She'd been the perfect wife for him, and until the shooting they'd never endured a serious conflict. How quickly and how permanently it had all been changed with the evil actions of one man.

Gray watched her surreptitiously as he drove. He'd kept an eye on her, of course, driving by the house daily to catch a glimpse, to make sure she looked healthy, to make sure, he admitted, that no other man was being received as a guest. Now he saw that she was as lovely as ever, small and dark with glossy hair that she never acknowledged as an asset but merely endured as a part of her anatomy. Despite her beauty, Lily had no vanity, which Gray had never understood. He had always loved to look at her, to feast on her visually, whether in the car like this or sitting at home watching a movie, or after making love to her, when she would lie trusting and open to him, relaxed in a way she never was during the day, smiling with shy acknowledgment of his ardor.

"Stop staring at me," she said, but not angrily.

"You're beautiful as ever," he said. "And as grouchy."

"I warned you about the grouchy before we got married."

The mention of marriage brought back the silence. Lily slouched at her window, munching on a granola bar. Gray sighed and, steering with his left hand, dug around Lily's backpack for a bag of pretzels. When he finally returned his attention to the rearview mirror, he realized something with a shock.

"Lily."

"What?" Her head turned swiftly at his tone.

"I think we're being followed."

THREE

"Lose them," Lily said.

"Okay, fine. I'm not Mannix, you know. I'm not Starsky and Hutch."

"Can you name any current TV cops?" she asked, peering out the back window. "What is it, the black Ford?"

"I think so. I noticed it back in Capitol City, but then when I made the turnoff, it just struck me. This is not a widely traveled road, not at this time of day, and that guy behind the wheel—"

"He looks like a goon," she said. She was trying to think, trying to tap into Danny's voice. What would he do if he were being followed? Surely he had spoken to her about this, all those hours that they'd spent driving around. He had been her main teacher, and he had taught with such humor—such love—that it had never been condescending.

"Why don't I just pull over and see what he does? If he pulls off, I can ask him—"

"*No!*" Lily hadn't been shaken by the news of a tail, but now she was agitated. Thoughts of Danny were too fresh in her mind. "That's a bad plan, Gray. You think I want to see another guy get shot right in front of my eyes? A guy going to confront a motorist he thinks isn't going to hurt him?"

Her face was pale, and Gray nodded his agreement. "Okay, I'm sorry. Not a good idea. But we can't have him following us to Halsted, so what do you suggest?"

Lily twisted the wrapper of her granola bar, her head bent into thinking position. "I guess you'll have to take the next exit at the last minute. It's not original, but it's all I'm coming up with right now."

"The Jeep will manage that better than his Ford, that's true," Gray said.

"Where's the next exit?"

"I think in about three miles. There, see that sign? Gas, lodging, Exit 38."

"Okay. That's our plan, and if he follows us, we'll think of something else."

They drove in a tense silence, Lily looking frequently behind to monitor the other vehicle. When the exit came up, Gray gauged it visually while maintaining his speed. Then, at the last possible moment, he turned the wheel hard right and squealed onto the ramp. The black Ford shot past on Gray's left, a blot in his peripheral vision.

"Good job," said Lily, trembling slightly. Gray pulled into a gas station lot, parked the car, and examined his tires. He got back in.

"It looks okay. The ol' Jeep is still roadworthy." He noted Lily's pallor. "Hey, are you okay? This isn't like you. You're my little toughie."

Lily closed her eyes and calmed her breathing through a gargantuan effort of will. She *had* been tough; she used to be unflappable. She'd been a great cop, Danny's protégée, his pride and joy. Gray had been proud, too. He had never minded that she was a strong woman. He wouldn't recognize her if she had one of her panic attacks now. They were misnamed, anyway. They didn't feel like panic; they felt like dying. "Your little toughie," she repeated wryly.

Gray reached out uncertainly. "Lily—um, do you need a hug?"

She flashed him a look that had him holding up a hand in surrender. "No," she said. She looked back out the window, staring at a gas pump until she was able to blink away all of the weak, weak tears.

Archie Halsted's cabin was on a wooded road that reminded Lily of the campgrounds of her youth, where she and her parents had once taken trips every summer, the family camper hitched to the back of their car. Houses and cabins peeked through the trees here and there, some of them with tidy trails of smoke curling out of their chimneys. The smell of wood smoke filled the air—a scent that Lily found both exuberant and sad.

She read the address from Gray's notepad, and he pulled the Jeep onto a gravel driveway that led to an unspectacular little building made of wood and painted pale blue. The latex was peeling, especially on the porch that they mounted moments later, and the place had an air of neglect that depressed Lily further.

The man who opened the door, though, had a friendly smile and a quiet manner, and the interior of the home he ushered them into was well kept if not glamorous. "Thank you for seeing us," Gray was saying, and he introduced himself and Lily.

"I read about you," Archie Halsted said to her, pushing wire-rim glasses up on his nose and running a hand through disheveled gray hair. "I'm sorry for your loss."

Very few people said this to Lily, because they never considered how much like family her partner might have been. People tended to forget Danny altogether when focusing on her, the one who had lived. She was moved to reach for the old man's hand. "Thank you," she said. "I appreciate it."

29

Halsted looked surprised. He nodded briskly, and Lily let go of him.

"Can I get you anything? I'm not stocked too well at the moment. I have some tomato juice, maybe some Dr. Pepper," he said, looking vaguely at his kitchen.

"No, thank you," Gray said. "If you'd be willing to sit down with us for a moment, we'd like to ask you some questions."

Halsted nodded, pointing with his chin to a table in the corner of the room. "Let's sit there." He held a paperback book in his hand, his finger still marking his page. He looked around until he spied something that looked to Lily like a bill, and stuck it into the novel with a bashful air. "John le Carré," he said. "Normally don't read that stuff, but he's got me, and I have to know what happens."

"You're retired?" Gray asked.

"Yes, sir. Didn't like it at first, but it suits me fine now."

"Was it a voluntary retirement?" Lily said.

Halsted's wooly eyebrows rose. "Well, yes. I was sixty-five, and I had my pension coming, so I took the package. It's a frugal living, but I've always been that way."

Gray and Lily exchanged a glance, wondering how to broach the topic. Halsted saved them the trouble. "You want to know about Emily Martin," he said.

"Yes, please," Lily answered.

"It was probably the strangest thing I'd ever encountered, but I didn't realize that at the time. You know how some things you just chalk up to office politics. People take over investigations, call them off, call them back on. We just do what we're told, basically. When Dr. Striker sent me the tissue sample, she asked me to run some standard tests. She wanted to know if there were any traces of gasoline or some other flammable substance. It would be natural, in this case. To determine if the car was burning before it went over or after."

"Right," Gray said. Lily nodded.

"I hadn't even started on the sample when I got a call from Dr. Striker, saying to destroy it. The investigation was off. She was having the body cremated."

Halsted drummed his fingers on the table. "I'm not normally the type that responds to tone or to nuance, but something there made me wonder if I shouldn't hold off to make sure this didn't come back to bite me. It had happened before. People change their minds, and a sample once destroyed is gone forever."

Lily leaned forward. "Did you tell anyone you saved the tissue?"

Halsted shook his head. "No. There was no one to tell, and I wouldn't have wanted to make it known, anyway. I put it away and forgot about it. I haven't really thought about it in years, until this young man called me." He indicated Gray with a wave of his hand.

Lily met Halsted's eyes. "The week before we were shot, my partner and I were looking into Emily's death. It was in our unsolved file, and we picked it at random. We had spent the week calling people, trying to find contacts, asking people about her—what she did the night of her death, that sort of thing."

"Stirring up the waters," Halsted said.

"Yes. That Friday we'd planned to interview her former employer. Thursday night we pulled over for what looked like a distress call, and we were both shot. There was nothing wrong with the car on the side of the road; it drove away after the shootings."

"They were stalked and executed," Gray said.

Halsted studied the spine of his paperback, deep in thought. "You want the sample. What for?"

Gray spoke. "We don't know. It's simply our only remaining link to Emily Martin, to what happened to her. I want to take it to an independent lab, have it tested, see if it tells us anything at all. The girl has been dead for seventeen years, but her preserved tissue may hold some clue to her murderer. It's a long shot, but—"

"It may not give you all that you need," he said. "Striker told me there was evidence in the corpse itself—within the cavity of the womb—of a fetus, perhaps a few months along."

"She was pregnant?" Lily asked, dumbfounded. None of her research had given any indication that Martin had been expecting a child: not the brief interviews with family, not the news accounts, not the medical files.

"I doubt that anyone knew," Halsted said.

"Except perhaps her murderer." Gray's words pierced the air.

"I'll get it for you," Halsted said simply.

He got up, creaking slightly, and almost fell down again when they both cried, "You have it *here*?"

Halsted blinked. "Where else? I don't work at the lab anymore. Didn't you read about that guy who kept Einstein's brain in jars in his house? Well, I have a few jars of my own down in the cellar there. Things I wanted to save or couldn't bring myself to destroy. Is that crazy?"

Lily grinned at Gray, suddenly euphoric. "Where else?" she repeated.

An hour later, after profuse thanks and a promise to let him know what transpired, they left the home of Archie Halsted with a little Igloo cooler in their possession: something that might normally contain a six-pack of beer but that held, in fact, the last mortal remains of Emily Martin.

Claudia Caldwell had never received such a strange phone call, certainly not from her own brother, and it was making her unusually nervous. She was a seasoned reporter and a popular anchor in Capitol City network news, partly because of her blonde good looks but mainly because of her professionalism. She had awards on her fireplace mantel to prove it. And yet she felt like a cub again when she walked into the press conference. She'd seen Nob Stevens before, talked with him even, and she had never found him intimidating. Yet the hands in her blazer pockets trembled while she talked with her sound man, and her eyes darted nervously to the door of the room where the governor was even now being prepped for his TV appearance. Everyone knew that he'd be announcing his candidacy for re-election today, and no one expected any surprises. Claudia forced herself to take a deep breath.

When Stevens took the stage moments later, she held up her microphone with everyone else, but she didn't join in the chaotic questioning that came afterward. She was too distracted. After the governor had left the building, after all of the hand shaking, photo ops, and general pomp and circumstance, she slipped away from Tony, her cameraman, saying she needed to use the washroom.

The makeup room was occupied only by the stylist, who had been on standby for touch-ups, and she was packing her things.

"Hi," Claudia said, walking forward with forced confidence.

"Hey, you're Claudia Caldwell," the woman said. "I watch your show. I like the way you and that cute guy joke around."

She was referring to Claudia's coanchor, Ben Stannard, who was said to have a "winning chemistry" with her on the air. They'd been voted the top news duo in Capitol City for two years running. She and Ben had found a great chemistry offscreen, too, for a while, but they had tired of each other soon enough in a relationship based solely on good looks and good ratings.

"Well, that's great," she said, stretching her lips into a smile. "How would you like an autographed picture?"

"Hey, I'd love that!" the stylist said, her eyes shining.

"Can I get something in return? It's really dumb, but my sister begged me to ask you."

33

"Sure. I mean, what is it?" asked the woman, leaning forward with great curiosity.

"Well, my sister is a huge news junkie, and she loves politics, and she has a giant crush on Governor Stevens."

"He is cute," the stylist said. "For an older guy. He has great hair."

"Well, that's the thing," Claudia continued, crossing her fingers in her pocket. "She loves his hair, too, and she asked me—isn't this crazy?—if I could get a lock of it for her. For her scrapbook. It's kind of nutty, but that's my sister."

"Well, how would I—"

"You know, just from the comb." Claudia indicated, with a dip of her head, the hard brush that the woman still held in her hand.

"Oh!" She looked down at the brush herself, as though this idea had never dawned on her. "Well, sure. Who cares, right?" She plucked several gray hairs from the teeth and handed them to Claudia, who removed an envelope from her pocket and stuck them inside.

"My crazy sister," she said, shaking her head and smiling in a confidential manner at the starstruck woman. "This is so great of you."

"Sure, sure. So do you need my name and address?"

"I'm sorry?" Claudia asked blankly.

"For the autographed picture."

"Oh! Right. Listen, here's one of my cards." She opened her little purse and pulled a business card from her wallet. "I'm writing the name of a girl on the back. Just tell her Claudia said to send you a picture of me and Ben and to give you a VIP pass to a taping. The girl you'll be talking to is Katinka."

"Katinka," the woman repeated. "That's a cute name."

"Hungarian," Claudia said, handing her the card and backing away. "Well, I appreciate your help, but my cameraman is waiting in the van for me. Thanks so much, and we'll see you at the station."

"Okay, Claudia," the woman called. "I'll keep watching your channel, for sure."

"Great," Claudia cried over her shoulder. God, she had never told so many lies, and the envelope felt hot in her pocket. Crazy sister, indeed. She didn't have a sister and she didn't have a boyfriend, but she did have a brother with a lot of explaining to do.

"We'll need to stay here for a while, until Paluzzi tells you what he thinks." Gray unlocked the door of his little apartment, the one in which he'd stayed since their separation. It was the basement of a house in Capitol City, a one-room space that the elderly owner rented out by the month. Lily had never been inside, but her heart lurched as she saw the spartan interior. This was how Gray had been living, without complaint.

Aside from a kitchenette in one corner and a small folding table on which he apparently ate his meals, there wasn't much to see: a bed here, a desk and chair there, a small television set on a table near the bed, a tiny bathroom hidden near the door. The place smacked of poverty; Gray had donated much of his pay to help Lily continue to cover the mortgage. Her private investigations didn't cut it, not after she'd paid for insurance and met the monthly bills.

"This place is horrible, Gray. I'm sorry," she said at once. "I didn't know." She turned to look at him. He was taller than she by a head; his brown hair was disheveled and needed trimming. He looked tired after their day of driving.

He shrugged. "It's kind of bad all around, isn't it, Lily? I'm not thinking you have it much better, even if you have a nicer house."

Gray had always been generous with his assumptions. Lily figured that, as the eldest child in his family, he'd learned to nurture his siblings and therefore to become a more understanding, more giving individual. She'd fallen in love with him because of it.

"Maybe after we get the all-clear from Paluzzi," she said, "you could move back in."

Gray froze in the act of taking off his jacket. His hands fell to his sides, and he looked closely at her. "Move back in? As your friend, or—"

"As my husband."

He closed the distance between them with long, swift legs. "Because you forgive me?"

"Do you think there was something to forgive?"

"Yes." His eyes were earnest. Lily felt a pang of love. She'd kept it at bay so long that she didn't know what to do with it. She felt a draft of autumn wind from Gray's poorly insulated basement window. It was a lonely moment.

"I still love you," she said in a rusty voice.

"Lily!"

"But I need to go slow. Really slow," she said, forcing a smile.

"Just a hug, Lily. That's all I want," he told her, wrapping his arms around her for the first time in half a year. "I just want you in my arms."

When Lily felt the familiar warmth, so long forbidden, a cold chunk at her core began to melt. It was healing, hugging Gray, and she nosed into the opening of his shirt to smell his skin. "Grayson," she said in a small voice.

"Baby, it's okay." He held her like that, easily, for a long time.

Lily breathed him in like oxygen.

FOUR

THEY STOPPED THE NEXT morning at Exeter Lab in Brompton, just outside of Capitol City. Gray's old college friend, a guy named Harvey, worked there, and they drove through an unfriendly drizzle to find the building. Gray ran inside and returned twenty minutes later without his cooler, smelling of rain and wet leather. "I had to call in a favor from Harvey and promise a dinner at home. With you and me," he said tentatively. "He wants to meet you, and you mentioned that we might—"

"That's fine," she said. She suppressed a smile. Gray was playing by her rules, more than she'd really expected. He'd offered to sleep on the floor the night before, but she'd insisted they could share the twin bed. They had, but it had been difficult, being so aware of each other, touching without loving. If he had once tried to kiss her, she might have given in, but she couldn't be the one to break the regulations, not when she was the one who'd made them. Her life was nothing without structure. Still, she'd been moved by his devotion, especially when she'd experienced one of her terrible dreams. She'd woken to find Gray's hand on her arm.

"Lily," he'd said. "You were having a nightmare."

"Huh?"

"You were swearing! It wasn't about me, was it?" He'd been joking, trying to calm her.

"No," she'd said. "It was just a dream, just—nothing." She couldn't talk about it, not to him. Being with Gray wasn't necessarily a good idea. Her life was full of choices; any wrong decision brought great risk.

Now she faced Gray's earnest query and nodded. "He's welcome to come. I'll make my spaghetti."

He sat for a moment without starting the car, and they watched rivulets of rain slide down the dashboard window in seemingly random patterns, like endless tears. Gray was smiling, though.

"Claudia called me this morning while you were in the shower. I asked her to get a DNA sample from Stevens."

"*What?*"

"She was at the press conference. I asked her to get a sample, anything she could think of, and she came through like a champ."

"How could she possibly . . . ?" Lily's mouth hung slack with astonishment.

"She asked for his hair. From the makeup lady. And she got it, Lily. She's got his hair in an envelope, and she's bringing it to Harvey in the lab today."

"So what will that do for us?"

"Maybe nothing. Probably nothing. It's not like that tissue is from Emily's fetus, so we can't necessarily determine if he's the father. But somehow I just wanted to cover all the bases."

"Because you're a scientist," she said softly.

"Yes, I guess that's why." He sent a probing look in her direction.

This had been a joke of theirs when they'd first started having sex. Gray had insisted that he needed to inspect her minutely, that as a scientist he could do no less. It was a gag that they'd referenced often in their bedroom, whenever his hands started roaming.

Lily's comment brought an instant heat inside the rainy car, and the windows began to steam. She stole a glance at him, then looked away. His eyes stayed with her, even when she closed her own, like a negative imprinted on her lids. In the rain today his irises looked silver.

He seemed about to reach toward her, so she shifted in her seat and cleared her throat. "It's Tuesday. Do you have to work today?"

"No. I requested some personal days after I talked with Halsted. I wanted to see you, and I hoped to pursue this a bit, so I cashed in some vacation time."

"That was nice of you. What do we do now?"

Gray brightened. "Well, if you're willing to work together, we could make a plan for the day. I was wondering: whoever went and talked to that nun, after you and Danny—well, did anyone follow up on it?"

Lily nodded. "It's a good question. I asked Tony, months later, and he said he'd sent someone out and the interview went nowhere. I doubt their hearts were in it. It was just a favor someone was doing for Tony."

"So we should go there."

"Good plan." Lily listened as Gray used his phone to call information and then the school. He clicked off his cell and turned to her. "Twelve o'clock. We can talk to Sister Jean Baptiste on her lunch break. Feel like having some breakfast in the meantime?"

"Are you paying?" Lily asked.

"If we go someplace cheap," he said, grinning.

"Then I would love to have breakfast with you," she told her husband, and, after a brief hesitation, she slipped her hand into his.

39

John Pierre stood before Nob Stevens, whom he had pulled away from a donor's brunch, his expression one of concern and apology. "There have been a few complications," he said.

"Son of a bitch," Stevens said, still smiling. "They'd better be little ones." He faced Pierre, hands on hips, enjoying his physical height advantage as a tool of intimidation.

"The husband was there—Grayson Caldwell. He was talking about how he was starting to believe her. I'm not sure what it meant; maybe he was just trying to get back in her bed. In any case, he was mumbling something about a man at some lab that was investigating Emily Martin's death—"

"There was no investigation," Stevens said, his smile gone.

"No, sir. But he mentioned something about a man named Halsted, and he mentioned that he believed you—killed—Emily Martin. Anyway, he was saying something about this lab technician, and then suddenly he said goodbye. Later that day our bugs were removed."

"Removed?"

"By the police."

"Fuck." Stevens dropped into a chair and stared at his hands. "What else?"

"One of our men tried to follow them. They left Capitol City together, late yesterday afternoon."

"And?"

"He lost them. That is, they tricked him with some fancy driving. Which means they were aware of the tail."

Stevens rubbed his eyes, then ran a big hand across his forehead as though to ease a deep pain. He leaned his skull against the overstuffed chair and scrutinized the ceiling. "John, we need to back off. They're aware of the bugs. They're aware of the surveillance. She might have even connected that to the mugger. She's not a stupid girl, or we wouldn't have this problem in the first place."

"I'm not sure I follow you, sir."

"What?" Stevens looked at him for a moment, then smiled. "Oh, sure. What I mean is, the girl has convictions. And she's stubborn. And clever. For all I know she could actually make the police believe this hogwash if she thought she had some circumstantial evidence. And now she's got hubby on her side. God, how people love to hang a politician."

Pierre nodded. That he knew to be the truth. "What's the next move, sir?"

Stevens contemplated Pierre for a moment, then leaped out of his chair and clamped a hand on the younger man's shoulder. "We stop giving the doofus squad the jobs that only my right-hand man can do."

"Sir?"

"You take over, John. In the field. I don't trust anyone else. I just want to know where she's going, what she's doing. You can keep a low profile, can't you?"

"I believe I can, sir."

"Now, let's just see what we can find out. I've got a golden campaign with no serious threats to my re-election, at least not in the form of candidates. I'm making money hand over fist. Those rich assholes out there just gave me another fifteen million for the coffers. So I can't have a girl with a persecution complex walking in with her bloody wounds like goddamn Banquo's ghost."

"I'm sorry, sir?"

"You never read Shakespeare in school?"

"Some, maybe. None that I remember."

"Good for you. Waste of brain power," Stevens said, clapping him on the back again. "Now let me get out there, and you make yourself a game plan. Don't know what I'd do without you, John. If all else fails, don't forget the concept of divide and conquer." With a final wave, Stevens disappeared, back to his political supporters, back to his two-hundred-dollar-a-plate champagne brunch.

John Pierre felt validated and proud; even more, he felt honored to be able to do something so noble as protect the governor. This girl, this Lily Caldwell, was perhaps not consciously vicious in her desire to implicate Nob Stevens. She was obviously ill, and a corner of Pierre's heart felt pity for her. It was his job, however, to see that her dementia did not interfere with a good man's campaign. John knew that he could do it. He was Governor Stevens's secret weapon, and even the governor didn't know just how loyal John Pierre could be.

Claudia arrived at the lab in Brompton on her lunch hour. She had sealed her envelope inside a Ziploc bag and put that in a plain brown lunch bag. She felt she couldn't hide those hairs enough, that they must be glowing through with radioactive light so that all the world would know what she had done. Then again, she thought, what had she really done? Asked for his hair. So what? There were people out there who probably did far worse. No one questioned those women who threw their underwear at Tom Jones.

She took a deep breath, stepped out of her car, and ran into the building. At the front desk she asked for Harvey. *Harvey*, she thought. *What a nerdy name.* Gray was going to owe her big-time for all this running around she was doing. Then again, it wasn't as though her brother hadn't done her favors. He'd moved all the heavy stuff into her new apartment. He'd come over and offered to get drunk with her when she and Ben had broken up. He'd asked her to stand up at his wedding. Now he and Lily had problems; it was bad enough that his wife had been shot and persecuted in the way that she had been. Now it all seemed to have taken a toll on Gray's marriage.

Claudia was brooding over this when a man arrived, a tall blond man with a sort of forest-ranger, outdoorsy look. He wore jeans and a black turtleneck. "Can I help you?" he asked with a pleasant smile. Nice teeth, she noted.

She smiled back. "I'm waiting for someone who works here."

"I work here."

Claudia cast him a doubtful glance. "I'm waiting for Harvey," she clarified.

"I'm Harvey. Harvey Janusek. And you're Claudia. I recognize you now."

"Oh?" she said, still gawking. "I'm sorry, but you just don't fit my preconceived notion of a scientist."

Harvey smiled. "You shouldn't have preconceived notions. Why don't you come back to my office? You can show me what you've got." Claudia raised her eyebrows, and he flashed those pearly whites again. "In the bag."

"Ah." She followed him down a carpeted hall. "So, is Mrs. Janusek glad that you work here?" It was the worst job of fishing that she'd ever done. No subtlety, no class.

Harvey led her into a small room with a cluttered desk and pointed at a chair. "Can I tell you how flattered I am that you want to know if I'm married? And the answer is no, there is no Mrs. Janusek. There was once, but there isn't now, and I'm feeling really glad about it at the moment." Claudia blushed; he'd rendered her speechless. "I like your style on the news. Breezy, but not silly. Serious when you should be. And I like that little lapel pin you always wear on those professional suits of yours."

She shifted in her chair. "You've really been paying attention."

"I have. Let's see your sample."

She took it out and handed him the Ziploc bag. He opened that, removed the envelope, and considered its contents. "Not a bad plunder. Whose hair are we examining here, anyway? The man you love?"

Claudia laughed. "Not hardly."

Harvey met her gaze with a pair of interesting green eyes. Something connected right then, and Claudia felt relieved. He put the envelope in a drawer. "I have to work a little late tonight, thanks to your brother. I'll have to work late for several nights, maybe. But I'll try to have the results back to him as soon as possible."

She stood up. "I'm sure he appreciates that, Mr. Janusek."

"Harvey, please."

"Harvey. Thanks for making time for this. I don't know the details, but I owed him a favor, and—"

"So did I. Now we'll both be even. And I've earned a free dinner for my troubles. Will you be there?"

Surprised, Claudia averted her eyes. "Uh . . . I don't know. I have yet to talk to Grayson at length."

"Well." Harvey acted brisk, standing up behind his desk. "Thanks for the delivery."

He shook her hand; Claudia pulled hers away and thanked him, then made her escape on impressively high heels. She heard his voice call after her, "And I hope to see you soon."

———

At another breakfast, across town, Lily was finishing a Belgian waffle with whipped cream. "It's good to see you eating," Gray said. "You weren't much for a while there."

"I feel good, Gray. You coming to me, telling me you believe me— it's done wonders for my outlook." He saw her smile as a gift, a glorious one. Her eyes were wide and bright with gratitude; Gray felt a tug of love, a string pulled inside him.

"I won't let you down again," he said, daring to wipe a tiny bit of cream from her upper lip. "There's not one damn thing that's going to come between us."

FIVE

SISTER JEAN BAPTISTE WASN'T what Lily expected. Not being a Catholic, Lily didn't know much about nuns, but she'd had a vague image of long habits and giant rosary beads that clacked with every motion. Instead she found herself across the paper-filled desk of what looked to be a busy executive: a woman with a no-nonsense hairstyle, gray and short; a pair of multicolor-framed reading glasses perched on the end of a long, sloping nose; and a pale pink power suit worn over an elegant gray silk blouse.

Lily introduced herself and Gray. She called him "my husband" and saw that it kindled something in his eyes. Her power over his emotions felt at once burdensome and addictive.

"I wondered if you would ever come here," Sister Jean Baptiste admitted the instant they were seated. "I remember our appointment, long ago, and I remember what happened. I'm sorry." Her voice was surprisingly firm beneath its gentle timbre, and Lily sensed a person of strength and purpose.

"Why did you wonder? Didn't the police send someone else?" Lily asked.

"They did. A couple of gentlemen came and asked me some questions. I sensed they weren't entirely clear of their mission. Your partner, Officer Donovan—he had seemed more certain of what he'd wanted, at least on the phone. I'm sorry I wasn't able to meet him."

Lily nodded, surprised at the sister's willingness to bring up subjects that were generally taboo. Then again, in Jean Baptiste's line of work, death wasn't considered a stigma. Lily paused, uncertain where she wanted to begin.

Gray leaned forward. "You have an excellent memory, Sister. Do you remember Emily Martin?"

Jean Baptiste opened a drawer and pulled out a Tupperware container. "Of course I do. Do you mind if I nibble? This is my lunch, and I might not get another chance."

Lily and Gray assured her that they did not mind, even as the smell of tuna filled the air. Lily was transported back to grade school and the lockers at the back of the room. They'd always reeked of tuna fish or peanut butter. She remembered, too, the smell of her leather book bag, blended always with the odor of fear, the terror of school itself.

The nun bit her sandwich and chewed for a moment, then said, "I was assistant principal back then. I've reviewed her file. Emily was a first-year teacher. She was a nice girl who had innovative ideas about teaching history. She had three sections of American history, a section of world, and a government class. Normally we don't ask a teacher to do three preps, but the scheduling just worked out that way."

"So there were no problems with her employment? You weren't displeased with her?"

"No, not at all. It came as quite a shock to us all when we heard of her death. As her colleagues we were particularly disturbed, because

47

we had seen her promise. And as I said, she was a nice, friendly person." She took another bite and waited for further questions.

Gray rubbed his hands together absently. "Do you know if she dated anyone? Had a boyfriend?"

Jean Baptiste nodded. "I'm fairly certain that she was serious with one of our other teachers. Roger Tallis. He still works here; he's the chairman of the English Department. He's married now, has four children." Her voice seemed to hold a warning: *Do not upset Mr. Tallis or his family*. Her face, however, was placid as she continued to eat her meager lunch.

Lily tried a different tack. "When you think of Emily Martin, what stands out in your memory? After seventeen years it must be only a few dominant images."

"You're right about that," she said. She took a baggie of carrots out of the drawer where the tuna had been, removed one, and crunched it thoughtfully. She swallowed politely before saying, "I suppose it would be the image of her parents. Their grief. Many of us attended the funeral, of course, and I spoke with them at length, especially her mother. Her name was—Camille? No, Camill*a*. She was a lovely woman, didn't even seem old enough to have a twenty-some-year-old daughter. But she was just loaded down with sadness; I thought there was something almost wild in her reaction. I remember thinking of those people who throw themselves into the grave, or the Indian wives who are expected to burn with their dead husbands. Suttee, isn't it called?"

Lily sensed there was something here; it was the first she'd really heard of family. "I tried to find Emily's parents. I couldn't track them down, and I wondered if they were dead," she said.

"No, I don't believe so. The mother had told me that she and her husband were going to move away, that Capitol City was too painful. Emily had been an only child, you know. I think the mother said Indiana. Perhaps somewhere near Indianapolis."

The phone on her desk rang, and the sound was so jarring that Lily jumped. Sister Jean Baptiste smiled apologetically before saying, "Yes, this is Jean Baptiste." She spoke for a while about a school matter, and Lily and Gray moved politely to the back of her office, where they compared notes in low tones.

"We need to talk to Tallis before we leave," Lily said.

"And we can hunt for the mom online, although . . ." Gray paused, his brows drawing together.

"What?"

"We need to talk to Paluzzi. They could have gotten into your computer and viewed everything that you did. We don't want them to know what you're doing from now on."

Lily gripped his arm. "Who are 'they'? Do you think Stevens is sending these people after me? Gray! That mugger had to be from him!"

"All right, I'm sorry," said Sister Jean Baptiste, hanging up the phone. "So much going on today. We have a pep rally later—our football team is doing quite well—and there are some little details to iron out before the assembly." She still seemed calm as she selected another carrot.

"Sister, I think we've taken enough of your time," Lily said, walking back to the desk and extending her hand. "I appreciate all the information you've given, and I thank you for your excellent power of recall."

The principal stood up behind her desk and shook Lily's hand, then Gray's. "It was no problem whatsoever. I hope you find what you're looking for regarding Emily. And if you suspect she was murdered, I hope you find her killer."

Lily stared for a moment. "Did I indicate that I was—"

"Your partner called it an unsolved case a year ago. I assumed there was the possibility of foul play." She raised her eyebrows and bit into the carrot she was still holding in her left hand.

Lily nodded. "There is more than a possibility, Sister."

"I can assure you that Roger is not a killer, but I've asked him to stop by. He knows why you're here. I'm afraid he can't stay long; he has a speaker coming to his class today, and he's running around and setting things up."

"We appreciate it," Lily said.

Sister Jean Baptiste nodded. "I was unhappy to hear of your firing. I believe it to be unjust. I hope you'll protest it, Mrs. Caldwell."

Lily was touched by the unexpected support; no one had ever championed her in the matter of her firing. Her mother, perhaps, but that was complicated by other things. Not even Gray, because by then their marriage had been in jeopardy. "Thank you so much, Sister. I may just do that when I finish this investigation," Lily said.

She turned toward the door, not sure where they were expected to wait for this Roger Tallis. She sent Gray a triumphant look; things were starting to go her way, and they both sensed it. Suddenly the door opened.

Roger Tallis was in his forties, balding, rather short, but pleasant looking in a former-athlete sort of way. He entered the room rather breathlessly, holding a file folder.

"Hello, Jean," he said, greeting his principal. He turned to Lily and Gray. "Roger Tallis," he said, slipping the folder under his arm and offering his hand.

"Mr. Tallis, we appreciate your coming to talk with us," Lily said.

"I'm afraid I can't talk long today; I didn't know you were coming. You can feel free to call me. I wrote my home number on this folder." He handed it to them with a slightly distracted air.

"And this is . . . ?" Lily asked, taking the file.

"When Emily died, the principal at the time, Father John O'Reilly, allowed me to sort through the things in her mailbox and her locker. I sent some of it to her family. Some of it just got tossed out: hand-outs and tests she would never give. And then there were some things I couldn't bring myself to toss, for sentimental reasons. Emily and I were romantically involved at the time." He smiled bashfully. "I was on the verge of proposing, as a matter of fact."

Lily peeked into the folder. Gray cleared his throat and asked, "Mr. Tallis, I wonder if I might walk you to your room and ask you just a couple more questions?"

Tallis raised his eyebrows. "Certainly."

Lily shook Tallis's hand, then watched the two men leave. She knew what Gray was doing: he wanted to ask about the fetus without involving Jean Baptiste. It was a good idea, and yet she felt a burst of resentment. Gray would have the information before she did. Gray, who until two days ago hadn't believed this investigation worth pursuing, was now as determined as Lily to find the truth. She had no monopoly on the information, and yet she felt she'd earned the right to it.

Even after she thanked the nun behind her and headed toward the exit and Gray's car, she felt the troublesome presence of a grudge she had thought was gone.

In this business, Lil, there will be people who want to steal your glory, people who want to climb over you on their way to the top. So every time you're successful, you've got to keep that pride in yourself. Sometimes you'll get your kudos and sometimes you won't, and you'll go nuts trying to compete. Just do your best, Lil, and be proud of yourself, and other people will recognize your value.

"I'll make *you* proud, Danny," Lily murmured as she sat in the car and paged through Tallis's file folder. There were a few memos there, written by Emily's hand. Some course syllabi and a few pages of lecture notes. Obviously Tallis would want these back as mementos. Two

51

pages were stuck together by what seemed to be an ancient coffee spill. Lily pulled them apart, and a little card that had been trapped between them fluttered into her lap. It was a business card for a Dr. Ian Worthington in Surrey, England. Lily flipped it over and saw only the word *Obstetrician* in what appeared to be the same writing she'd seen on the notes. Emily's writing.

"Hmm," she said as Gray opened the driver's door and climbed back into the car.

"What's that?" he asked.

"What did Tallis say?" she countered quickly.

Gray looked surprised. "He admits the baby was most likely his. They'd been sleeping together. He seemed very sad to learn of the child. He'd thought all this time that he'd lost only a girlfriend—bad enough. I feel rotten, being the bearer of that news."

The sight of Gray's real compassion made Lily feel mean for holding back. She handed Gray the card.

"Obstetrician," he mused. He handed it back to her, and she replaced it in the file.

"Why?" Lily asked. "He's in England. Was she going to have him deliver her baby? Were American doctors not good enough? Was she going to move across the sea?"

Gray shrugged. "Curiouser and curiouser."

"Let's go," Lily said. "Back to my place."

By the sudden clenching of his hands on the wheel, Lily saw that he'd noticed her choice of possessive pronoun and that he wasn't pleased.

Paluzzi yelled into the phone, as if Lily couldn't hear him well enough already. "You tell me what's going on, Lily," he demanded, "or I'll come over there myself and get it out of you in person. That was sophisticated stuff you had in your house, and I want to know who put it there."

Lily felt a burst of indignation. "So do I, Tony! That's why I called you. My hunch is that the governor paid someone to watch me, but I'm not sure how he knows what I suspect. Maybe a cop leaked it to him. That would make sense, wouldn't it, Tony?" she asked. "No, wait, of course not, because none of you believe me. So I guess some other wealthy person with access to nice surveillance equipment decided to case my house for no particular reason. It's certainly none of the lowlifes I've been working with as a freelancer."

She scowled her frustration at Gray, who had walked into the living room with a bowl of popcorn. He set it in front of her, and she grabbed a handful. It was nice to see Gray in the house again; he'd packed a small suitcase and come home with her after Paluzzi's secretary had told them that their home was free of investigators and of bugs. Now Paluzzi was on the horn and as confrontational as ever, although Lily knew that it was concern that sent his voice into a higher pitch and raised his volume to the rafters. "Lily, you been hunting down this governor thing?" he asked.

"You know I have," she said. "I never lied about it, Tony. I said I'd find my evidence."

"And did you? Have you found any evidence like you said?" Lily hesitated, and he pounced. "You tell me, dammit!"

"Only recently," she said. "It's still nothing I can prove, but we're on a trail. Gray is on it with me, and he believes me now."

"Goddammit," Paluzzi barked. "Let's say it's true. You're going to get yourself killed, like Danny did."

"No," Lily said calmly. "If I was meant to die over this, I would have died last year, on that table. Or on the street where he left me. I was meant to hunt this down for Danny, and that's what I'm going to do."

"Dammit," Paluzzi said, but he was losing steam. "Okay, okay. What do you want me to do?"

Lily shook her head, as if to dislodge the confusion, and pulled on the lobe of her ear. "What? What do you mean, what—"

"You heard me. God—what sort of help do you need?" His tone was the height of exasperation, but Lily saw through it, and she started to cry.

Gray took the phone. "What did you say, Chief? You got her all choked up."

Paluzzi sighed in Gray's ear. "I'm offering help, a year too late. Better late than never. Tell her to call me if she thinks of something."

"I will," Gray said, his brows raised. He hung up the phone and looked at Lily, who was punching the life out of a throw pillow.

"I'm turning into a total wimp," she said, aiming her blows with precision. "First, I let you come walking back in, even after you broke my heart." Thud, thud.

Gray said nothing. "Then," she continued, "I start blubbering to Paluzzi, just to reinforce his image of me as a little daughterly girl."

"He loves you," Gray said, sitting down next to her. "And I do. Maybe you just had the wisdom to see that. Leave that poor pillow alone."

She flung the pillow away and turned to him with a pugnacious expression. "You didn't stand by me, Gray."

"I know," he said. "Have I told you that I'm sorry?" His hand slipped into the silk of her hair, and she closed her eyes.

"Yes," she said.

"Have I told you that I love you?"

"Yes."

"I'm glad to be home, Lily. It's where I belong." His hand slipped down to her neck, and he cupped its slenderness in his curved palm. "With you. With my wife."

Lily leaned toward him, eyes still closed. "Maybe it is," she whispered.

She felt his lips before they touched hers, felt their nearness and the slight breath from his nostrils cooling her skin. His lips were warm, though, and six months hadn't lessened their ability to render her limp, helpless, full of a swirling desire that found release in a sudden cry against his mouth. "Gray," she said. So many feelings were vying for her attention that she didn't know what to think or what to do. The one that surfaced, though, was that she wanted him.

His little grunt of surprise and pleasure only encouraged her, and she pressed herself against him, no longer willing to be strong if it meant pushing him away. She reveled in the feelings that she'd denied herself—denied him—for months. She smiled as his tongue teased her lips and then pressed through them to seek hers. She clutched the back of his head, suddenly wanting him as close as he could be.

His mouth covered her with kisses, both repentant and seductive. His lips slid over her face, her earlobe, her neck. He tugged at her academy sweatshirt, and she lifted her arms so that he could pull it over her head. Then that moment of silence, that instant of tension, as he observed her scar, not yet white but still pink with the memory of blood and pain, shaped like a flower between her breasts and soft to the touch in a different way from the rest of her skin, petal pink and petal soft. Beneath it trailed the mark of her incision, a stem for the bloom above. Gray followed it with a gentle finger until it disappeared inside her bra. "It's changed," he said. "It looks different. Better. It's almost beautiful."

Lily shrugged. "I'm used to it. Will it bother you?"

He shook his head. "No. Only as a reminder of what you suffered. Nothing could make you less beautiful to me." He pushed her gently backward and they lay down together on the couch. His mouth descended to touch her scar gently, lovingly, then traveled down, suddenly impatient at the cleft of her breasts. He tugged at her brassiere and flung it aside, then closed his eyes and let his lips remember her, all of her: the soft skin, the generous breasts, the nipples that hardened beneath his tongue.

Lily sighed with relief and pleasure. She hadn't wanted him to go; she hadn't wanted to lose him from her life. She had merely wanted his belief. Now she had it, along with his contrition, and she thought it was going to be enough. Nothing in her life had been perfect, but much had been good, and if she had expected Gray to be faultless, then she would need to show remorse as well.

She helped him remove her jeans, and they made quick work of his own T-shirt and sweatpants. The feeling of his skin on hers was more healing than all of her therapy sessions with Dr. Alvarez and more pleasurable than anything she had known since the shooting. She'd lost a year of her life to grief and numbness, and in the last day she'd felt much of her life come flooding back, the good feeling and the belief that things could be the way they once were.

Gray entered her gently, carefully, whispering endearments. She wrapped her arms and legs around him like wings of forgiveness.

———————

"I was starting to think—to fear—that we would never be together again," he said later, his mouth against her ear.

"Gray, I'm glad you're back. So glad. And I'm sorry, too."

He lifted his head in surprise. "For what?"

"You've always been perfect to me. And all that stress—it was yours, too, not just mine, and no one could be without fault in those conditions. I wanted you to be, and I hated you for being human. I hated you." She touched his brows, his nose, his mouth with a tentative finger. "I'm sorry for that, because you were only good to me."

"We forgive each other. And we just showed it." He nestled against her, his face in her hair, kissing lazily.

"Oh!" Lily said.

"What?" His mouth stopped its motion.

Her pills. Her birth control pills. She'd thrown them out when she'd thrown Gray out. She hadn't intended to need them ever again, or him, or any man. It had been months since she'd thought of the pills, and their lovemaking had always happened so naturally that this time she had forgotten that when they had been together before she had taken steps to protect them from pregnancy.

"What is it?" Gray repeated.

Lily looked into his warm eyes and felt the familiar pain and pleasure that was love. "Nothing," she said. "We'll be all right, Gray."

SIX

She was back in the rain, squatting behind the car. She could see Danny, lying immobile on the wet concrete; the moisture was reflected in the light of the squad car's headlights. Suddenly Danny turned to look at her, expressionlessly, not pleading or laughing, just there, alive. "Danny!" she cried. "You're okay! God, Danny, I've been so worried, thinking you were dead! I've got to tell Tony. We've got to get you to the hospital!"

"Watch out," Danny said, and even from that distance, in the dark, she thought a tear ran down his craggy face. She turned, and a man was there, a silver-haired man, smiling, polite. Behind him were reporters, taking pictures.

"This won't hurt," the man said, pushing her back on the concrete, pulling at her belt, putting her weapon aside. She looked at it longingly. It was right next to her, but she couldn't take it, somehow. She'd lost all control. She heard Danny in the background, calling, "Get me to the hospital, Lil. Lil, I'm dying!" But the man stood over her, smiling, pulling at her pants.

"Don't mind the reporters. They won't know," he said, even as the flashbulbs burst, blinding Lily. "It will be our secret, yours and mine. Be sure you don't tell anyone."

"No!" Lily cried in sudden anguish, but her body remained still, unmoving under his violating hands. "No!" She was screaming, crying, trying to drown out the sound of Danny's pain, and even as she cried she heard the stranger's laughter, felt his utter lack of response to her suffering, to Danny's agony. "You bastard!" she shrieked.

"Lily?" Gray was there, pressed against her in the bed. "What's wrong? Are you dreaming again?"

"What?" Lily was still half-asleep, not sure why she felt so terrible.

"You were dreaming. You were having another nightmare. Do you still have them?"

She shook her head and rubbed her face. "I don't know."

"Oh, Lily. My poor baby." He hugged her to him. "Do you want to talk about it?" he asked.

"No," she said shortly. "I mean, thanks, but I don't want to talk about it."

"I'm here when you do," he said. His arms were warm and draped over her, comforting as a hot-water bottle.

She leaned into him and closed her eyes. She feared sleep, feared the return to that nightmare world that had become so familiar to her. To sleep, perchance to dream . . .

Danny had liked that play, *Hamlet*. He knew the "To be or not to be" soliloquy. He'd performed it in a variety show at his church. *Well, Danny, it was not to be*, she thought, as hot tears pooled in her eyes. She fell asleep with her back to Gray, unable or perhaps unwilling to share the burden of her sorrow.

Linda Stevens sat on her bed, reading a fashion magazine. She despised the premise of these magazines, these little snippets of nothing that were supposed to enhance a woman's life. *What colors suit you? What body shape are you? What turns him on?* Suddenly disheartened, she flung the magazine aside. As a former model she supposed she should have a certain interest in what other people in the industry were doing and what they looked like. She didn't care. She had never liked modeling—only the money it brought her when she was forced to live on her own.

When she'd met Nob, she'd felt she had a chance at what she considered a "real" life: a home and a family and stability with a man who worked to make the world a better place.

Now here she was. She contemplated herself in her dressing-table mirror. At forty she was still beautiful, with strawberry blonde hair and blue eyes that had graced more than a few covers when she was in her prime. She'd expected, in all those months when she'd been hoping and praying that Nob would propose, that she would be happy sitting here. What she noted most about the face in the mirror, though, was the desolation.

She heard Nob coming and walked slowly to the bed, like a woman in a dream.

She heard him enter the room, felt him staring at her in that disturbing way he had. "Hey, Lin," he said, pulling at his tie. "You look mighty scrumptious tonight."

"Thanks, Nob." She reclaimed the magazine and flicked pages, trying to show that she was tired and uninterested.

He came closer, shedding clothes as he went. "What you got under that robe, babe?" he asked.

"Oh, Nob. I thought you had some sort of business dinner tonight."

"Cancelled. Rescheduled. Lucky me, huh?" He eased onto the bed and slid himself against her, touching her with heavy hands, without finesse.

"Nob, honey, I don't know if I—"

"Linda, we talked about this! How are we ever going to make that baby we want if you're always pushing me away? Don't you want a baby, hmm?" He planted his lips on her throat, and his hands pushed her robe off of her shoulders, revealing her thin nightgown.

"Nob, yes, of course I do. I'd love a baby. It's just—I don't want you to be upset with me if—"

"Not tonight, Lin. Not tonight. I'm really wanting you. I've been picturing you all day, picturing your pretty face, your beautiful skin, your gorgeous body." His hands were busy as he spoke, undressing her, flinging away the clothing. He seemed not to notice her total lack of cooperation in the process, nor was he offended by her failure to respond in kind and undress him. He did it for himself, and soon he was heavily on top of her, pulling at her breasts with greedy fingers, kissing her mouth with moist passion. "Yeah, baby, that's what I like," he said as she summoned up the energy to wiggle beneath him.

She eased her head to the side, allowing his kisses to go on without her. She was waiting; it always happened now, as he began to reach fever pitch, as she felt him rubbing against her, as he tried to insinuate himself between her legs. She would hear him curse, some horrible word, and he would lunge off of the bed in a fury of frustration. Once, in the intensity of his disappointment, he had slapped her.

Tonight, however, even as she squinted her lovely blue eyes in anticipation of the storm, she felt something quite different. Her husband was inside her, actually inside her, and he was grunting his satisfaction into her ear. Her astonishment was so great that she gasped with something like pleasure.

"You like that?" he asked.

"Nob, oh—yes! Make love to me."

To her great surprise, he did.

———————

Lily woke the next day to find Gray in the corner of their bedroom, working on the computer that Paluzzi had lent them while Lily's was being examined. She sat up and smiled at him, rubbing at her eyes. "Hello," she said.

"Hello, pretty. Don't you look sexy today, with your crazy hair and that little smile."

"I suppose I just look happy. What are you doing?"

Gray stood up and walked to her, some printouts in his hand. "You've got two e-mails. Do you mind that I read them?"

"No." She slipped out of bed and ran to the little bathroom in the corner. "Wait till I brush my teeth, in case you were planning to kiss me."

"I was," he said. "But I shall be happy to wait. Lily, do you want to talk about the dream you—"

"No." She peered around the corner, softening the word with a rueful smile. "No. But thanks, Gray." She went back in, avoiding his worried look.

"Who's the first one from?" she called from the bathroom.

"Paluzzi. He says there's still no trace of the Martin file, but he's trying to get some information back for you."

"That's nice," she said through a mouthful of toothpaste.

"The second one is from Tallis. He says he doesn't recall ever seeing the business card for Dr. Ian Worthington, but he thinks she might have asked him where Surrey was a day or two before she died."

Lily came out of the bathroom, clad only in a long T-shirt. "An obstetrician. Why, Gray?" Gray pulled her to him and kissed her soundly. "Why don't we send him an e-mail and ask him?"

"A brilliant idea. You know, I have a spying job to do today. Sorry—investigation. I just feel like a spy. Unless I can get out of it. I might be able to farm it out."

Gray ran a hand down her arm. She noted that he couldn't seem to stop touching her.

"I think you should," he said. "I want to spend this time with you, even if we spend it hunting clues about Emily Martin. I want it to be just us."

"Mmm," she said, pulling his head down for another kiss. "Then I will. I'll call Paul Ostrowski. He works nights, so he might want a little day job. The money's good. He has kids."

"Good. Let's go lie on the bed for a while," Gray said, his voice thickening slightly.

Lily giggled, then stopped as he tried to pull her there. "Gray, wait. I want to tell you something."

"What?" He was tensed for a blow, and she felt the pain of it. It was the sudden realization that she had hurt him, that he bore his own scars, that made her push him down, sit in his lap, and look into his gentle eyes.

"I'm not on the pill. I didn't think I'd need it, and then yesterday and last night, well—we weren't protected. And if we do this now, we won't be now, either."

He gazed at her for a long moment, and then his grip tightened, as though he feared she'd fly away. He said carefully, "I don't care. Do you care, Lily?"

Strangely enough, it was Danny's voice that entered into this most private of moments, telling her that trust was intrinsic: *You can know when you look someone in the eye, Lil. You know at that moment of connection whether you can trust him or not. It's not in the academy handbook, but it's true.*

Lily looked in Gray's eyes. "No, I don't care."

63

He pulled her down with him, and she sank almost gratefully.

Later, her nakedness twined with his, she sighed silkily and said, "You know what I missed, Gray? Your French toast. Would you make French toast today?"

His laughter echoed through the house like a blessing.

Lily sent the following e-mail to Dr. Ian Worthington:

Dear Dr. Worthington,

My name is Lily Caldwell. I am a private investigator and former police officer in Capitol City, in the USA. I am looking into the death of a girl named Emily Jane Martin, who died under mysterious circumstances in October of 1989. Your business card was found in her work mailbox, and I am contacting you in the hopes that you might remember Miss Martin and her affiliation, if any, with you. Might she have been a former patient, for example? Miss Martin was only twenty-three years old when she died, and her mother and father were devastated, since Emily was an only child. If you can shed any light at all on the matter, or if you might be able to explain why your card was in her possession, I would be happy to hear from you. I am enclosing my home phone number, as well as my e-mail address, for your convenience. Thank you for your time.

Sincerely,
Lily Caldwell

After she sent the letter, she wrote a quick e-mail to Tony Paluzzi as well, which read as follows:

Dear Tony,

Now that you're actually treating me like a sane individual, I do have a favor to ask. Can you tell me the whereabouts of Emily Martin's mother and father? Sister J.B. thought they'd moved somewhere near Indianapolis. Gray and I couldn't find any listing online this morning. Yes, we slept together. Get over it.

Lily

Paluzzi read the e-mail twenty minutes later, while he was munching on a power bar at his desk. He laughed right out loud and said, "Oh, God. She's back."

John Pierre pulled away from the curb in an inconspicuous white Ford. He kept a sedate distance while following Grayson Caldwell's Jeep. The two were obviously back together, he thought. They were hanging all over each other when they emerged from the house; instinctively Pierre knew that the governor wouldn't like to hear that. Obviously he preferred to think of Lily Caldwell as an isolated threat, a woman without connections. Looking at her, Pierre couldn't believe she was considered a threat at all. She looked more like a cheerleader than an ex-cop; she couldn't be more than a few inches over five feet.

Still, Pierre knew, any allegation made against a person in power could damage that person's career, and so Lily Caldwell could not be considered negligible. Governor Stevens had not earned his exalted position by making mistakes about people like Lily. Pierre felt a surge of admiration for his employer as he stopped at a red light. In the Jeep he could see the heads of the Caldwells coming together while they waited for the light to change. Yes, definitely a reunion, and that meant two people to watch. He only hoped they stayed in the same place so that surveillance would be possible. Right now they led him to a grocery store; they went inside briefly and came out with a bag, presumably, Pierre thought, with some breakfast in it.

He took out his little tape recorder and spoke into it, recording the day, the time, and his mission. Pierre had aspirations in government himself, prompted by his surprising promotion and his perception that it wouldn't be so difficult to stay at the top if he stayed on his toes. He believed that, most importantly, he needed to be quiet and observe. He rarely spoke unless he was spoken to, but his recorder was the exception. Pierre recorded everything.

Lily ate Gray's French toast, for which he'd purchased his signature ingredients of cinnamon and pumpkin pie spice, with great enthusiasm.

"So what now?" she asked after checking her e-mail in box and finding it empty. "We haven't heard from your friend Harvey, we haven't heard from Tony, we haven't heard from Ian Worthington, and we can't contact the Martins. Where do we go from here? I hate waiting."

Gray walked up behind her and put his hands on her shoulders. "Harvey said he'd put a rush on it. But it's a complex process. He'll be using STR profiling, which—"

"I remember that term from the rape trial where Danny and I had to testify. What's the STR again?" She swiveled to face him, so he squatted in front of her and put his hands on her lap.

"Short Tandem Repeat. It's a very sensitive test developed for forensic analysis."

"But he can't really learn if Stevens is the father of Emily's child."

Gray shook his head. "Not unless he determines he has tissue from two individuals in the sample. If that were the case, then he'd have the sources he needed to establish paternity."

"How?" She sparkled at him, and Gray was pleased to note she was interested in the science behind the investigation.

"Well, a small amount of each sample is treated to release its DNA. An enzyme is used to copy the genetic code at certain variable regions in the DNA. Then this is repeated over and over to produce several million copies for analysis and comparison. He would color-code the results with a dye, a fluorescent dye. Remember when the lawyer at the trial mentioned electrophoresis? That's when the results are separated and detected by a laser."

"Okay," she said, playing with his hands.

"Then he'll get an STR profile, generated by his computer. It displays the results as a graphical trace—"

"But it needs three samples: mom, dad, baby."

"Mother is not required to determine paternity."

Lily threw down his hands. "Then we'll get nothing, Gray, after all this chasing around! We have mother but not baby."

He sighed. Archie Halsted had seemed like an important lead, but Lily was probably right. He stood up. "My legs were starting to hurt, although I'd love to kneel at your feet all day."

Lily grinned. "As you should."

"But there's plenty we can do. The first thing, I think, is to meet with Claudia."

"Why?"

"She has access to the governor, at least every once in a while. Do you want to try to get access to him, too? Or would you like to send a message through her?"

"No, Gray. I'm not going to involve her anymore. She jeopardized her career just with the hair thing. You shouldn't even consider it. But we should thank her. Maybe invite her for dinner or something. Hey, you said you had to give Harvey dinner. We can invite them together. What's he like, anyway?"

Lily's face had brightened with the thought of matchmaking. Gray's heart throbbed with hope. She was so different since he'd mentioned Halsted, so happy again. What if nothing came of it? Would she retreat from him, as she had before?

"He's ugly but appealing," he joked. "He couldn't make it to our wedding, otherwise I'm sure you'd remember—"

"And he's only recently back in town, right?"

"Yeah. I sort of reconnected with him last month."

"So would he be good for Claudia?"

"We'll see," he told her. "But maybe I should call—"

The phone rang then, and they stared guiltily at each other, as if this weren't a normal occurrence. Lily answered, then handed it to Gray.

"It's Harvey," she told him, her eyes wide.

Gray took the phone with a sudden surge of adrenaline. He paced as he talked. "Harvey," he said.

"Gray, you owe me big-time. This is a pricey test, and I stayed quite late working on it, but I assume you'll be happy with the results."

"What results?" Gray asked. "Were you able to determine if there was any fetal tissue—"

"There was only one person's tissue in the sample. However, your daddy sample matches your kid sample. There was a sort of strange— well, anyway. We won't go into that now." Harvey's voice, as usual, was lighthearted.

"What? A match?"

"Well, with 99.9 percent accuracy. You know the drill. So when's dinner?"

"What?" Gray was staring at Lily, whose face grew white as she regarded his.

"When's dinner? The wonderful dinner in a happy home, cooked by you and the beautiful goddess that you call your wife."

"Uh . . . right. Dinner is tonight, I think. We'll have my sister here, too, if you don't mind. We might need to form a brain trust."

"Your sister? God, she's a lovely creature. Do you mind if I harbor dirty thoughts about her?"

Gray was too distracted to be insulted. "Just date her like a normal human being," he said. "I have to go. Dinner's at seven. You know where I live?" He gave Harvey some brief directions, then hung up the phone.

Lily grabbed his arm. "What is it? What is it?"

He grappled with the knowledge that he'd gotten and decided that it was good. He smiled at her. "We got an answer, Lily. It's positive."

"Nob Stevens was the father of Emily's baby?" Lily asked hopefully.

"Nob Stevens was the father of *Emily*," he corrected.

SEVEN

Linda Stevens jogged back into her bedroom to retrieve her purse. She was about to run errands—some shopping and a trip to the dry cleaner. Nob always wanted her to delegate those sorts of tasks, but she missed them. She missed being a young girl-about-town, independent and in charge of her own day. As the governor's wife she sometimes felt on display, but in a different way from modeling. As a model she'd been judged sexually. As Nob's wife she felt she was constantly evaluated as a human being—and often found to be wanting. She longed to escape into anonymity, into her past, which she hadn't realized was good until she looked back at it from the confines of the governor's mansion.

Sometimes, too, she remembered Joshua and the alternate life he had offered her. Had she made the right decision? She'd thought so at the time, but lately Josh was on her mind more and more, and her day-dreaming was distracting her from daily life. She was at an impasse: Should she see a therapist? Discuss her feelings with Nob? Leave Nob? Seek out Joshua? Or would going somewhere alone for a while solve the problems that she had trouble elucidating? It wasn't just Nob's impotence, she told herself. She wasn't that shallow a woman. Nob was somehow emotionally unavailable, even when they weren't in bed. At first, at the beginning, she'd tried to talk to him, tried to cajole a response from him. But she'd found a curiously childish tendency in him to simply walk away from her, sometimes while she was talking. If she tried to share her feelings, he'd shake his head and refuse to respond.

She didn't have any experience in marriage, but she felt it was wrong of him to invalidate her emotions the way he did. Nob made it so that she always felt guilty in the end. He was manipulative, a talented spin doctor. She supposed that's how he'd won the election in the first place. She had been naive, she realized, to assume that her life with him would be all sophistication and glamour. The reality of their four years together was that he was gone often, and when he was home they had an unfulfilling sex life and nothing much to talk about.

She sighed, hunting for her handbag with growing frustration. She looked under the big bed that sat centrally in their large, plush room. She glanced into the closet even though she knew she hadn't been in there. She walked into its depths, admiring her long line of clothing and Nob's equally impressive sartorial display on the other side. The suit jacket he'd worn the day before was hanging slightly askew; automatically she pulled down the hanger and readjusted the expensive jacket. Nob could be careless about his clothes.

Something thick slapped against her leg as she turned the hanger. She felt the pocket and realized that Nob had forgotten something. *A book?* she wondered as she reached into the silk-lined depths and pulled out a yellow envelope. She hung the jacket up and carried the envelope into the bedroom. She would leave it on Nob's dresser so that he wouldn't forget about it.

She walked across the plush white carpeting of their room—carpeting she never would have chosen but also never had to clean—and was about to set the packet down when her curiosity got the better of her.

71

She was thinking of Pandora when she opened the flap. She tried to hearken back to the mythology she'd learned in school . . . why wasn't she supposed to open the box? Linda knew that it was the troubles of man that had emerged, that Pandora had been given the chance not to open it. It had always interested her, that story. *I'll have to look it up,* she thought, and she pulled a pile of photographs out of the envelope, along with a letter.

The photos were shocking, but Linda attributed it to the naiveté that she had lately identified in herself. She'd once considered herself a woman of the world, but the older she got, the less she felt she understood. She turned her attention to the letter and read it through, a cold feeling spreading through her. She didn't believe it. She read it again, then looked back at the pictures. Her shock was like a drug, pillowing her, protecting her from a reality too monstrous to bear.

Carefully, she returned the pictures to the envelope, making sure the letter was exactly as it had been, and walked on trembling legs back into the closet, where she placed the entire package back in Nob's pocket. She smoothed the flap down with careful fingers, then walked out again, where she stood in the center of the room, seeing nothing. She hadn't even identified her primary emotion before the nausea came, rising so quickly that she had only seconds to run into her gleaming bathroom, drop to her knees, and throw up into the elegant, pale gray porcelain.

Nob arrived home late; he never tired of being driven through the gates of the governor's mansion, of walking boldly up the stairs of that imposing structure and calling it his own. Since childhood Nob had known he'd wanted wealth, and his path had always seemed clear before him. He possessed a singular talent for transforming his desires into reality; he always had. There was only one thing he hadn't gotten, and in that he'd been forced to concede defeat. Somewhere beneath his present pride and confidence lay a residue of bitterness from that loss.

He strode into his foyer, had some words with the security guard on duty, spoke with his housekeeper about a late dinner, and then marched up the stairs in search of his wife. Yesterday's lovemaking had given him renewed assurance, and he intended to repeat the experience as often as possible, being a strong proponent of the "use it or lose it" mentality.

He found Linda in her study, a pretty, airy room with wide windows, where she liked to attend to her correspondence. She was on the phone. She looked pale, almost ghostly, and he felt annoyed that the pallor was so aesthetically unpleasing against her distinctly colored hair.

"I have to go," he heard her say hoarsely. "I'll call you back. Nob is here now."

She replaced the receiver in its cradle.

Nob noticed her reluctance to meet his eyes and grinned. She obviously felt shy after last night, when he'd ravaged her and brought her such pleasure.

"Hey, Lin," he said. "Come on down and have some dinner with me." He turned back toward the door, confident that she would follow.

"Nob." He barely heard her. She had to clear her throat and start again. "Nob, that was Stella."

God. Linda's sister. Nob didn't like her, never had. "Oh?" He didn't bother to sound pleasant.

"She's sick, Nob. She has cancer. She's going to start chemo tomorrow. At first she wasn't going to tell me, but . . ." She shrugged, still staring at her lap. "I'd like to go there, to be with her." Her eyes darted up to his, then flicked back down, shy and deferential as a geisha.

Nob bit back his first retort, but he blew out some angry air. Finally he said, "Lin, this isn't a good time. I've got that fundraiser next week, as well as the luncheon that you're supposed to be in charge of. The fundraiser is a big photo op, and it's understood that people want to see my wife. I'm not the photogenic one, Lin. You're the former model. You know how many votes I probably got because of that fact alone? Because you looked better on my arm than Stan Hendry's wife looked on his? Besides, after last night, I'd think you'd want to stick around—"

"I know, Nob, but it's never a convenient time to get cancer. We'll just release a statement to the press, saying I have a family health issue to attend to. It won't be for long, anyway, I'm sure. Just to get her through this first round, or at least the first couple weeks of it." Linda was making a fan out of her skirt, folding it this way and that, almost nervously, Nob thought. She wasn't acting like herself, but he supposed he could attribute that to the shock of the news she'd received.

Nob sighed noisily, making her feel the full brunt of his disappointment and displeasure. "When would you want to leave?"

"Well—tonight, Nob."

"No." His response was immediate, and he realized he'd been looking forward to going to bed with her more than he'd known. "Go in the morning. At least let me be with you one more night, Lin." He stepped forward, intending to persuade her with a kiss and a caress.

She leaped up so quickly he stopped in surprise. "No!" Her blue eyes flashed at him, then her lids covered them as she looked down in apology. "I mean, she's in such emotional pain, Nob. I need to be there for her. What sort of sister would I be? She's only got me now, really, with Mom gone and Dad so far away. Please let me go to her, Nob. I'll make it up to you."

This was the first interesting thing he'd heard her say. "How?" he asked.

She shook her head, still looking down, her nostrils flaring slightly. "I—uh, I don't know. Whatever you'd like."

"You mean in bed?"

She lifted her head and met his gaze, but it seemed to cost her something. He'd never realized how devoted she was to Stella. "Of course, if that's what you want. You can—think about it, what you'd like, while I'm gone." Her smile was ghastly, but Nob didn't think of that until later, when it was too late.

He sighed again, martyred. "All right, all right, if you have to. Call up Sanderson. Tell him we need to talk PR. He can come out and have a drink with me after dinner. You joining me?"

She nodded. "I'll make the call, and then I'll come down. Maybe have a bite." She lifted the phone again, a slight tremor in her normally steady hand.

Nob eyed her warily. Her behavior was strange, but it could all be explained by her sister's cancer. And yet . . .

"All right. Listen, I'm sorry about Stella. I'll see you downstairs," he said, and he walked briskly away.

His footsteps made no sound on the plush carpet, so he could still hear her voice, elegant and modulated, saying, "Yes. Bill Sanderson, please."

––––––––

"You're saying the *who* did the *what* now?" Harvey asked in disbelief, his spaghetti momentarily forgotten.

Gray broke off a piece of garlic bread, perfectly calm. "Needless to say, Harv, this doesn't leave this room or go beyond us four people."

"Naturally," Harvey said, his green eyes wide, "since no one would believe it, anyway."

"Tell me about it," mumbled Lily, toying with her food. The four of them had shared a nice, friendly dinner, and she sensed that there was, in fact, some interest between Harvey and Claudia. She and Gray had decided that they needed more people on their side. Obviously Claudia, being family, was trustworthy; Harvey had gone to college with Gray, and the two of them had attended church together on Sundays. Gray had told her, before Harvey arrived, that he would trust his old friend with his life.

So here they were. Gray had told both of their guests about Lily's vision, and now they waited to see how much they were believed. Claudia looked thoughtful. "I've interviewed people like you, Lily. People who came back from death with knowledge they hadn't possessed in life. It's a fascinating idea, that you were given the identity of your would-be murderer."

"But do you think I'm crazy, like everyone else?" Lily asked.

"Why would I? Plenty of politicians are involved in scandals and cover-ups. It's hard to believe anyone you've met before is a murderer, but it happens all the time. I doubt I'll ever look at him the same way again. Good thing I got the hair before you told me what it was for."

Harvey choked on the food he had just placed in his mouth. He coughed, holding up a finger, and eventually recovered enough to say, "Are you telling me that was Governor Stevens's DNA I was testing? And you got it without his permission?"

"That's right," Claudia said coolly. "He certainly wouldn't have given his permission, so that was the only way."

Harvey pushed his plate away. He wasn't finished eating. Lily saw that as a bad sign. "What exactly are we trying to prove here, folks?" he asked quietly.

Gray said, "You already did prove it, Harvey. Governor Stevens was the father of the girl Lily was investigating when she and Danny were shot. Governor Stevens had something to do with the death of his daughter. And with the suppression of any investigation. And the disappearance of the file that Lily and Danny had been working with."

"Why would anyone kill his own offspring?" Lily asked. The idea had been plaguing her ever since Gray had told her the DNA results. "It just doesn't make sense."

Claudia shook her head. "It doesn't seem to, but there's at least one person in every jail who's done it. Look at all the cases you see on the news—Susan Smith, Andrea Yates, Scott Petersen. Now imagine all the cases you don't see."

Harvey looked unconvinced. "Okay, I've proved he's her father. But it doesn't sound to me like you've proved anything else. This is dangerous, trying to take down someone so powerful." He looked troubled; Claudia gave him a searching glance.

Lily nodded. "You're right, we haven't proved it, but we're getting there, Harvey. And we need some help from some trustworthy people. We want to know if the two of you will support us."

Harvey looked at her closely. "If you really believe it's true, and you've gone a year with nothing happening, no one paying the consequences—God, it must feel like murder *and* rape."

The awkward silence at the table and the refusal of anyone to meet his eyes told him he'd said something inappropriate. Harvey looked around uncertainly, hoping someone would enlighten him. "Did I say something—"

Lily interrupted him. "It's okay, Harvey. Gray and Claudia know that I was raped once, so they feel uncomfortable that you said that. But it's really okay. One of the things we learned in counseling is that it's all right to say the word out loud. And I'll tell you something. You're right. Rape makes a victim feel powerless, makes her feel rage and frustration, because somehow, somehow, she feels she should have prevented it. But I'm an exception, I guess, because I always knew where to place the blame, and it wasn't on me. That helped me recover. But this thing with Governor Stevens? It's worse. Because I still feel helpless. I still feel he's abusing me, every day that he gets away with Danny's blood on his hands."

Harvey took her hand across the table, and, to Lily's relief, there was no pity in his face, but rather a good deal of admiration. "I like you, Lily," was all he said.

Lily's rape had happened years before, when she was nineteen. She'd lived with her mother, and her mother's boyfriend, Fred, had begun living with them, too. Lily hadn't liked him from the start, but she hadn't known how to express it to her mom, especially because she'd felt that if she told the truth, her mother might have told her to leave. She'd been out of high school and working; she could have potentially lived on her own. It was her mother's house, her mother's life. So she'd said nothing about Fred, the boyfriend, and kept her dislike to herself. Then one night when her mother was at, of all things, a cake-decorating class, Fred walked right into Lily's bedroom, where she sat painting her toenails and listening to the radio.

He pushed her back on the bed, spilling her pink nail varnish on her coverlet. The stain never came out, and later Lily threw the bedspread away. She never polished her nails again; she couldn't stand the smell.

He hadn't been apologetic; he simply pinned her down, told her she was pretty, said he'd always wanted her. She struggled, silent at first with shock, and then became more vocal as he started to ease up her nightgown. He covered her mouth with one hand and opened her legs with his knee.

One of the many random thoughts that came to Lily later was that she wished the light hadn't been on; it seemed to lend the whole scene a sense of normalcy that it hadn't possessed, and her memories of it were that much brighter.

When Fred finished, he stood up and walked out of the room, leaving her with a warning that she should say nothing to anyone about, as he put it, "what happened between us." He went into the living room and began to watch TV.

Since Lily had been a child, she'd admired the police. Once, as a little girl, she'd played with the phone and accidentally dialed 911; when a uniformed officer appeared at the door minutes later, Lily regarded her with awe. To be a person who responded to a distress call, to wear a handsome uniform and a belt full of equipment, to carry a gun that you would use, if necessary, against evil—Lily thought it was the most remarkable thing she had ever seen. Her fascination with police officers grew from that point, and her parents had bought her a little doll who sat in her own police car and wore a similar handsome uniform.

After Fred raped her, she had no qualms, as some victims do, about her own falsely perceived complicity in the matter. It was his fault, and it was rape, and she would make him pay. Shocked, horrified, yet calm, she crawled to the phone at her bedside and dialed 911. "I've been raped," she whispered into the receiver. "My mother's boyfriend just raped me."

Her admiration of the police was enhanced that night; though she knew that some rape victims had terrible experiences, either because they were treated as promiscuous or partially culpable or simply not human, her rape had been handled appropriately. Within minutes Fred was in handcuffs and being read his rights; Lily was approached by a female officer, Officer Hardy, who asked her gentle questions and accompanied her to the hospital, holding her hand and telling her she was sorry about what Fred had done. When Lily's examination was over, Officer Hardy drove her back home and gave her the name of a counselor, then spoke with her mother, who had returned to an empty house and still clutched her pastry bag and spatula in her hands, her face white from learning of two separate horrors.

Lily had begun counseling the next day and had entered the police academy six months later. Her mother had apologized endlessly for what Fred had done, blaming herself for bringing him into the house. Lily verbally forgave her, but things between them were never the same after that point. She did, in fact, see her mother as an inadvertent accomplice to the crime: first, for divorcing Lily's father (who had since died); second, for feeling it necessary to replace him; and finally, for choosing someone as unacceptable as Fred.

When Lily took the job in Capitol City, she thought her mother was sad yet relieved to be farther away from her daughter's reproachful eyes. Lily knew that her condemnation of her mother wasn't fair, but she couldn't bring herself to feel any other way. Fred had been arrested, but he had served only one year in prison for what he'd done. Her mother, ultimately, hadn't protected her, and Lily couldn't forget.

She'd come to Lily's wedding, of course. She hadn't been invited to anything else. When Lily was shot, her mother had sent a barrelful of red roses. She'd called, when Lily could talk, and asked if she could come out to see her.

"I've been so worried, honey," her mother said.

"There would be no point, Mom," Lily answered. "I just lie here. Maybe later, when I can walk around. That would be a better time."

"Of course," her mother agreed. "There would be no point."

But Lily had heard the pain in her voice, had understood that she was causing a wound in her mother that was similar to her own—torn up around the heart. She'd finally relented and, knowing that her mother wanted desperately to help and to make amends for Lily's second tragedy, had asked her to come out and make meals for Gray, assist with cleaning the house, and just be with him for a week or so. Jenny Mason had done it gladly, and when she'd walked in the door of the hospital room and rushed to Lily's side, Lily had burst into tears.

She brought herself back to the dinner table, where Claudia was saying, "When someone is a celebrity, you simply can't imagine him committing a crime."

"Like O.J.?" asked Gray dryly.

"Plus, wouldn't he have some henchman do it for him?" asked Harvey. "I mean, are you sure it was him, Lily, and not just some representative of him?"

"It was him," Lily said. "And what if he was protecting a secret that even his henchmen could not know? Maybe there was a reason no one could know that Emily was related to him. Or maybe his daughter witnessed something that she wasn't supposed to see. Or maybe he killed her accidentally in a family squabble and then put her into the car and sent it off the road."

"But in the news accounts," Claudia said, "was there any mention of her having a famous father?"

"No," Lily said. "Everyone assumed the Martins were her parents. But now we know that at least one of them isn't—Mr. Martin. Maybe Mrs. Martin isn't, either. Maybe Emily was adopted and had recently found out that Nob was her father."

"So he killed her?" Harvey said, not believing it.

"I don't know," Lily said. She looked across at Gray. "We're being bad hosts. Does anyone want more spaghetti? Or should we clear this for coffee and dessert?"

"Oh, dessert," Harvey moaned. "God, I'm no better than when we were in college, Gray, and always desperate for cookies." He stole a glance at Claudia. "Did you ever visit Gray at school? I think I would have remembered you."

"I was twelve," she said wryly. "And I don't remember you."

"Oh, the pain," Harvey said, clutching at his heart theatrically.

Lily began stacking plates. "The point is, we need a game plan from here. We need to know how to proceed, and we need your advice, the brilliant scientist and the savvy reporter."

Claudia regarded her soberly. "You can't afford to make any mistakes, Lily."

"I know." Lily touched a place near her heart, where her scar sat like a warning on her skin. "But I think I learned enough from Danny to know when I'm doing the right thing." She blushed slightly but lifted her chin, almost defiantly.

Claudia and Harvey looked suitably moved. Gray wouldn't meet her eyes.

EIGHT

Nob Stevens finished his late-night brandy and realized he was nodding over his papers. He put them aside, stretched, and walked wearily to the door of his first-floor study. In the hall the security guard sat like a prison sentry, stone-faced and burly.

"Everything go all right? With Mrs. Stevens?" Nob asked.

"Yes, sir. She left at about nine forty-five." The man stood deferentially to address Nob.

"Who drove her?"

"I'm sorry, sir?"

"Who drove her to her sister's house?"

"Mrs. Stevens was picked up, sir. She said the arrangements were all made."

Nob's brow furrowed. "Why in the hell would she have them pick her up when we have a perfectly—" He broke off. He didn't like to show emotion around the staff.

He stomped back into the study and went to the phone. If they didn't like him calling this late, they should have made the plans clear, he thought grimly. He dialed the phone with a vengeful finger.

"Hello?" Stella's voice, still awake.

"Stella, it's Nob." He turned on the charm for her, despite his anger. "Just wanted to check if Linda got there okay."

"What—Nob? I'm sorry, I'm not following you. Was Linda coming out here tonight?"

For a frozen moment Nob studied a book that sat on his desk: *The Rise and Fall of the Roman Empire*. The title made him angry; suddenly everything in his line of vision was making him furious: the desk, the bookshelves, the curtains, the ceiling—

"Excuse, me, Stella, there must have been some miscommunication. May I ask, did you speak with Linda earlier tonight?"

"Why—no, Nob. I don't think I've talked to her in—"

"And how's your health been? Linda mentioned a cancer scare?"

"Cancer? My God, no! Knock on wood." Stella's voice was growing more and more curious, and slightly alarmed. Perhaps she feared he was drunk. "Nob, is everything all—"

"Oh, it's fine, it's fine. I'll have Linda call you tomorrow. Sorry to bother you so late. Good night, now." He hung up without waiting for a response.

His fists clenched as his mind rapidly went through the possibilities. There had been something wrong—he'd sensed it at the time—but she'd had a story prepared to explain her reactions of . . . what? Had she been afraid of him? Certainly she had kept a physical distance and had barely looked him in the eye. The night before, everything had been fine. She'd been pleased, very pleased, when he'd made love to her. So what had changed?

A possibility crawled into the back of his mind, unwelcome but impossible to ignore. He bolted from his chair, crossed the room in a few strides, and flung open the door. He faced the security man. "Mrs. Stevens made a call sometime around eight o'clock. Find out who she was calling."

"Yes, sir."

Nob moved swiftly up the stairs. He was barely conscious of the steps that led him to his bedroom, to the giant closet, to the patting of his suit coats until he found the right one. His fingers felt the bulky package, and he removed it from the pocket. The pictures were there, all there, and the letter. But were the pages in the right order? Had Linda seen this?

He walked back to his bed and sank down on it. The photos of Camilla distracted him. It had been her, always her, whom he loved, and he'd unearthed the pictures the day before in a sudden longing for her. He'd even looked at them at work, read the letter over and over and admired her familiar, spidery handwriting. It was this more than anything that had inspired him to successfully make love to Linda, these pictures of a woman long lost to him. The pictures were nudes, all of them, many taken while she'd been sleeping but some while she was awake—and therefore under duress. He liked those the best.

He forced himself to put them away, though he would have liked to sit and gaze at them for hours. If Linda had seen them, if Linda had read the letter, then Linda was a problem, a huge problem. *God*, he thought, *women are going to be the death of me. Camilla, and Linda, and Emily, and this Lily Caldwell. All women who don't know their place.*

He sighed heavily, his head bowed. There was a knock at the door. "Yes?"

The security guard entered. "Sir, the call was made to a Joshua Randall. His address is listed at—"

"I'm familiar with Mr. Randall. Thank you," he said.

The guard exited, and Nob felt a brief spasm of hope. Could it be that Linda had merely left him for another man? Josh Randall had been his rival for her affections. He'd never expected Josh to win, but women were unpredictable. He went swiftly to his bedside phone and pulled Linda's personal address book out of her nightstand. He found Randall's number and dialed it with hasty fingers.

He listened to the ringing phone; finally Randall's voice came on the answering machine. "You've reached the home and studio of Joshua Randall. Due to a family situation, I will be out of town for an indefinite period of time. You can reach my secretary, Hazel White, at—"

"Shit," Nob said, hanging up. "Shit." If Linda had left him, that was one thing. If Linda and this man had left town, that was another. She didn't want to be found, because she knew that Nob would want to find her. Like a fool he'd let her pack a bag and walk out right under his nose, let her ex-boyfriend come sailing up to the house to pick her up and take her to some undisclosed location. To a safe house.

At no point since he was nineteen had Nob ever felt that he was not in control of his destiny, of the events in his life. Now the feeling was back, and it was alien to him. He shook his head, shrugged it off, and reached for the phone. Linda was too gentle—too nice. She was no match for Nob Stevens, even if she had won the initial skirmish. The light of battle was in his eyes as he barked, "Get me Pierre."

Lily checked her e-mail late Wednesday night and found an answer from Tony.

Mr. and Mrs. George Martin lived in a house in Indianapolis. The street address and phone number were attached. At the bottom of the missive he obviously hadn't been able to resist typing, "Be Careful."

Gray came up behind her, sliding his arms around her waist and kissing her neck.

"Look at this," she said.

He read it and gave her a squeeze. "So it looks like we're taking a trip tomorrow. A long one."

"We could probably go by train," she said. "It would be faster, and we could take a cab from the station."

"If she agrees to see us," Gray said.

"Even if she doesn't," said Lily.

NINE

"Linda?" Josh asked it softly, tentatively. They'd arrived at his uncle's vacation home late the night before; he'd shown Linda to her room with nothing more than a compassionate squeeze of the arm, and now she sat with her morning coffee, staring out the window.

She turned at the sound of his voice. She forced a smile for him. "I didn't thank you last night," she said. "You must have thought me so presumptuous, calling you out of the blue after four years. Asking for such a giant favor. You must have thought—"

"I thought you needed me, and I was glad," he said, sitting down beside her. "Do you want to talk about this?"

She shook her head. "Not yet. And the thing is . . . no, I can't really believe that, but—well, I don't want to put you in any danger."

"Danger? From Nob Stevens?" Josh grinned at her. "Are you telling me he's corrupt?"

Linda set down her coffee and met his eyes. Her expression must have been pathetic; his hands reached for her, offering comfort.

"Oh, Josh," she said, and she came to him, her tears dampening the shoulder of his denim shirt.

She stole a glance at him, and for the first time since she'd gotten into his car the night before, she saw something like apprehension in his eyes.

"So you want me to switch my attentions to Mrs. Stevens?" asked John Pierre's voice, surprised.

"First things first," said the governor, still hearty despite the sleep deprivation that showed on his face. "My wife and I had a misunderstanding, so I must find her to clear it up. I can't have her worrying over something that isn't true. You see what I'm saying?"

"Yes, sir."

"My wife takes priority. Plus we don't want it getting out that she took a little vacation. I need to know where that vacation is, and you have to find that out through Randall."

"Her old friend."

"That's right." Stevens stood up behind his desk and glanced at his watch. "I'll put someone else on the Caldwells for now. You find Linda for me, and I'll take it from there."

Pierre rang off, and Nob sighed. With Linda taking up his time and Pierre unable to keep an eye on the Caldwell girl, he'd been forced to do something rather drastic, a Plan B he'd held in reserve for quite some time. He needed Lily Caldwell out of his hair, and he'd made sure she would be, at least for a day. He grinned in spite of himself. Yes, Linda was a complication, but knowing what Lily had in store cheered him considerably. *Nob Stevens, two*, he thought. *Lily Caldwell, zero.*

Thursday morning Lily stood in her kitchen, contemplating the withered leaves in her front yard. Last week they'd been orange and red, aflame with the passion of dying. Now they were just dead. Gray came up behind her. She felt his presence like a powerful shadow. He put his arms around her, and she closed her eyes briefly.

"I'm going to make a grocery run. Our larder is bare," he said.

"My larder, you mean." Lily opened her eyes, staring again at the leaves.

Gray's hands tightened on her waist. "No, I meant ours, Lily. Do you see me as just visiting?" He spun her around.

Lily forced a laugh. "No, what I meant is that two days ago I was still on my own, and you are subtly criticizing my ability to . . . provide."

"I'm just saying that we need groceries, Lily."

"It felt like it was more than that."

Gray's hands slipped off her arms, and he took a step back. "That's because you're feeling defensive. And maybe you're not as willing to forgive me as I thought. So you're looking for reasons to be angry with me."

"I'm just questioning your implications." Even as she said it she felt its falseness and recognized her own perverse desire to hurt him, because somehow she felt guilty for allowing his presence. Gray was right, but she wasn't willing to say that out loud.

She saw the change in his posture, saw the stiff, almost embarrassed fumbling for the pad on her table. "Is this the list?" he asked.

"Yeah." She wanted him to embrace her again; she wanted to start the scene over. The damage, though, was done; she saw it in the weariness of Gray's expression. "Add milk to it," she said.

"Sure." He headed for the door, avoiding eye contact.

"Gray . . . ," she said.

"I'll be back soon, Lily."

She watched him walk to his Jeep, young and trim in his jeans and turtleneck. He was beautiful to her, even in discord. She wanted him back. It would break her heart if he left again, but letting him in was painful, too. She found she wasn't very practiced at forgiveness.

She sank into a kitchen chair and pursued that thought. She'd never forgiven anyone. Not her mother, certainly not Fred, not Paluzzi or Gray. Not even her father or Danny, who'd had the audacity to die, neither of them with the courtesy of a goodbye. She'd been convinced that she was in the right and that forgiveness was not her obligation. Now she wasn't so sure. She felt herself pushing Gray away almost as determinedly as she'd pulled him back. Was she doing it, she wondered, so that when he left her again she could place the blame squarely on him?

Tears came unbidden, and Lily's lip curled in self-deprecation. She never used to cry. Now the water flowed with every stress in her life. She stood, wiped at her tear ducts, and was headed toward her computer to continue her endless quest to destroy Nob Stevens when she noticed the cruiser. It sat in front of her house. She saw no evidence of a driver, but had that car been there when Gray left?

The doorbell rang, and Lily jumped. For the first time in her life, she felt a certain dread of the police. It couldn't be good, she thought, for that car to be there.

She opened the door to see two officers she knew—Sharon Gonzalez and Hughie Deutsch—in uniform, unsmiling.

"Lily," Sharon said by way of greeting. They'd been friends, seen movies together, shared tubs of ice cream. Sharon had a no-good boyfriend named Eddie that she spoke of endlessly to Lily. Lily had Gray, and she had felt flattered that Sharon wanted to confide in her, the old married woman, the happily married one. Sharon hadn't called since the firing, though.

"Hey, Sharon. Hughie," Lily said. "What's going on?"

Hughie shrugged, uncomfortable. He was more of an acquaintance, but a couple of times when Lily had car trouble he'd given her a ride to work, talking at length about his beagle, which he entered in dog shows with some success.

"Yeah, howya doin', Lily?" Hughie said, looking past her into her hallway. "We have to ask you a coupla questions."

Lily stared. "What—is it about the mugging? Marvin said he'd get back to me about the—"

She saw by their blank expressions that they weren't calling for that reason. "Questions about what?" she asked.

Sharon looked pained. "Where were you last night, Lil?"

Lily felt it like a blow to the stomach. She'd asked a thousand potential perps that question: *Where were you last night, Mr. Reynolds, when your wife was assaulted? Where were you, Miss Olivarez, when your neighbor's things were stolen?*

Now, after the indignity of firing, came this. "Where was I? Why? What happened last night?"

Sharon and Hughie exchanged a glance. "You been pretty upset with Tony, Lil?"

Lily stiffened. "Did something happen to Tony? Is he hurt?"

Sharon gave her a searching glance. "Lil, I need to know the truth now. This is hard enough. You telling me you didn't smash up Tony's car last night?"

Lily's laughter was both relieved and angry. "Someone vandalized the chief's car and you come here? Before the druggies and the pimps, you go to Lily Caldwell, because she might be holding a grudge? And when have you ever known me to tell a lie, Sharon?"

"That's not why we're here," Hughie said, his face red.

They have something on me, Lily thought. *But what? How?* She cleared her throat. "I was here last night, with my husband and his sister and a friend. Three witnesses."

Hughie took out a pad. "How long were they here?"

She sighed, suddenly near tears again, horrible, betraying tears. "Claudia and Harvey left around eleven, eleven thirty. Gray stayed."

Sharon's eyes darted here and there, not resting. "I heard Gray didn't live here anymore."

That didn't surprise Lily, but she felt a stab of resentment that Sharon had known about the end of her marriage and hadn't called to commiserate. She had an image of their days chatting on the couch, eating cookie-dough ice cream and waxing poetic about the wonders of chocolate. She lifted her chin, half-defiant, half-embarrassed. "He stayed all night. You want corroboration, he's at Sam's Club on Central."

Sharon shifted on her feet, and Hughie put away his pad. "We'll do that, Lil. Come on with us now. We need to ask you some questions downtown."

Lily's jaw fell. "Are you arresting me? Is this an arrest?"

Hughie looked almost sick. "Only if it has to be, Lily."

The three of them stared at each other, not one of them happy. Finally Lily shrugged wearily. "Can I get my purse? And some shoes?"

"Of course," Sharon said angrily.

For the first time in her life, Lily rode in the back of a cruiser. Even after her rape, Officer Hardy had made certain that Lily sat in front, never wanting her to feel as though she'd done anything wrong.

Now she contemplated the backs of the heads of these police officers, listened to the familiar squawk of the radio, smelled the staleness of Hughie's cigarettes. "So did Tony send you here for me?"

Sharon shook her head. "He probably knows by now, Lil, but it came down from somewhere after the computer match came in."

"Computer match? What—are you talking prints?"

Sharon nodded, not turning around. "Baseball bat left at the scene. Your prints all over it, Lil."

Lily laughed, long and hard, nearing hysteria. She knew what she was dealing with now, which meant she might not be going home as quickly as she'd hoped. Finally she calmed herself, wiped away tears of mirth. "Eleven years on the force and you guys think I'd leave a clue like that behind? It's a plant, for God's sake!"

She saw Hughie's eyes in the rearview. There it was again. Pity. She didn't even bother to see if Sharon's expression matched her partner's.

This was Nob Stevens's doing, and wasn't he clever? Because it would make her look even more like a lunatic to deny that she slammed Tony's car with a baseball bat. She had motive, of course; Tony had fired her. Now, if she returned to the station and blamed this on the governor, too, she would appear certifiable.

Where, she wondered, had he gotten her prints? He could have done it anytime. Maybe when his henchmen planted the bugs, they took up a print sample for use later, for something like this. It was easy enough to do it; all they would have needed was a piece of tape and a likely print. Perhaps they had a more sophisticated way of doing it. How many other people had Nob Stevens framed?

She nodded, almost smiling. He was clever, she gave him that. The fact that he'd made a move, however, made her see that he felt more threatened than he had before. Maybe she was making progress; maybe it was really happening. If only it didn't feel so much like an illusion.

They neared the station, and Lily clenched her fists.

"You look me in the eye and tell me you think I bashed in your car," Lily said quietly, staring Tony Paluzzi down.

Tony shifted in his chair. "What do you want me to do? We've got your prints, we—"

Lily slouched in her chair and glared at him. She felt like an angry teenager, misunderstood by the world of adults. Perhaps Tony saw her that way, too. "You know who did this," she said. "You just won't believe it, because it would mean believing me."

Tony slammed his hands down on his blotter, making her jump. "I tell you I'll help you, and then this happens!"

"Right! It doesn't make any sense! Why would I hurt your precious Volvo?"

Tony stared, the temper dying in his eyes. "I sold the Volvo three months ago. It's a Mustang now. Red."

Lily raised her eyebrows. "Sounds nice. I've never seen it, Tony."

He leaned his head back. "Goddamn."

"There's something else you should know, unofficially." Lily looked at her nails.

"Don't tell me anything unofficial. I don't want to hear it."

"Nob Stevens is the father of Emily Martin."

"Goddammit, don't you dare tell me how you—"

"Gray got a DNA sample of his hair, and we matched it with a tissue sample of Emily Martin, a sample we traced to a scientist from Gray's lab, a guy who worked there back when Emily died."

Paluzzi's eyes bulged. "You can't—you're not—you can't just—for fuck's sake!"

Lily felt suddenly serene. "He knows that I know. This is his little diversion."

Tony buried his face in his hands. "Either you're in deep shit or you are totally nutso."

Lily stood up and went to his desk, standing in front of it until he looked at her. "Which one do you think, Tony?"

————

By the time Gray got home his depression had left him. Of course Lily would still have her moments of doubt; it wasn't his role to fight her, but rather to prove that he was worthy, that he would stand by her even when she used her anger to push him away. He felt a sense of urgency. He wanted to see her, hold her, tell her he understood. He hauled four bags from the car and brought them all to the door. He didn't want to fumble for the key; he rang the bell with his elbow and waited for Lily to assist him.

She didn't come, and a burst of anger surged back. "Dammit, Lily, my hands are full! Open the door!" he yelled.

Nothing happened. With an oath, he set down the bags and hunted for his key. He opened the door to an empty kitchen. *Is she that angry with me?* he wondered as he went back for the groceries. It was only after he had set the bags on the counter and closed the door behind him that he saw the note on the table, written in Lily's endearingly sloppy cursive. A moment of sheer panic seized him. He didn't want to lose her again; he didn't want this to be a goodbye.

He picked it up, dreading it, and read:

Dear Gray,

I'm sorry for what I said. Of course they're our groceries. I know I'm hard to live with right now, but that's what you get for coming back. I need you to love me, even when I'm mean.

On an unrelated subject, the police are here and asking me to answer questions down at the station. It seems Tony's car was vandalized last night, so Lily is the prime suspect. I'm not sure if I'm under arrest or not. If I am, maybe you can bail me out.

Do you believe this, Gray?

She didn't sign the letter. In her final words he read desperation, despair. Another betrayal for her to endure. "Shit," he said, and reached for the phone. He dialed the number he still knew by heart and barked at the receptionist. "Tony Paluzzi. And don't put me on hold."

TEN

"Governor Stevens has asked me to find Mrs. Linda Stevens, who has disappeared for reasons known only to the governor. I assume there is some marital squabble behind it, but obviously the governor doesn't want it made known to the public, with his candidacy in such—"

John Pierre flipped off the tape recorder. He wondered, suddenly, if all politicians had so many emergencies. Lily Caldwell, Gray Caldwell, some anonymous man in the coroner's office, and now Mrs. Stevens. It was strange . . .

His cell phone rang. "Sir?" he asked.

"What's happening?" asked the governor.

"I'm going to talk to Randall's secretary, see if I can find out where he went."

"Fine. Get back to me immediately when you find out."

"But won't you be tied up with all of those school visits?"

"Get back to me immediately."

"Yes, sir. If the secretary doesn't know, then I'll—"

"She knows. Make her talk."

"Yes, sir."

The governor hung up. John Pierre looked at his phone for a moment, as though it would clarify the jumbled thoughts in his mind. It was more a feeling that came over him, really, and he wasn't accustomed to those. He pulled his car into the parking lot of Joshua Randall's studio. He stared at the door of the building, a bright red in the center of the clean brick.

He thought of Linda Stevens. She was beautiful, but he'd ceased to be intimidated by that years ago. The fact was that Mrs. Stevens was good, even kind, beneath her glamorous exterior. When Pierre had made a mistake once and forgotten to pick her up at a time the governor had instructed, he'd arrived an hour late and in a panic. She'd climbed into his car with an assortment of shopping bags and a mischievous expression. "Oh, John," she'd said, winking at him. "Your mistake gave me an extra hour of play time. So let's neither one of us mention this to Nob."

She had been lying, of course—he'd obviously inconvenienced her—but she'd been moved, he thought, by his genuine panic, by the sweat that poured from his brow.

More importantly now, he reflected on what he'd seen the night before. He was there when Linda Stevens left her house; he'd been pulling up in his Ford with a late-night report about Lily Caldwell, and he'd seen her approaching a black Cadillac.

He waved. She paused. His car pulled up next to the Cadillac under the portico, and he found her right next to his window. He rolled it down. "Evening, Mrs. Stevens." He had always been devoted to her, but especially so since the time she'd saved him.

She hesitated, darting a glance at the front door of the mansion. "Good evening, John. You're here so late."

"Just a final conference. Glad to see you're getting away from it all." He grinned, implying only that she was going to have some fun, reduce her stress. It was the kind of thing people said all the time.

Her expression had become suddenly hunted. There was no other word for it. Now, thinking back, he had the chills.

"You have a nice evening, John," she said, but she wasn't smiling.

Pierre had barely noticed the driver of the car, but he'd been surprised when she'd gotten into the front seat. It was only later that it registered in his mind that she'd been carrying not only a purse but a suitcase as well.

Pierre was twenty-nine years old and experiencing his very first crisis of conscience. He'd decided, ever since his one and only run-in with the law, to live on the straight and narrow, and he'd done it. He'd been proud of his reputation in the governor's office, proud of the governor's need for him. His conscience had told him that he should help a good man, whatever it took. Trust, though, was like faith, Pierre realized vaguely. It was there inexplicably, and just as inexplicably it could vanish. Now he was at an impasse in his young life.

He had trusted the governor implicitly for four years, and now, in an instant, he didn't trust him anymore.

———————

Gray burst into Paluzzi's office without knocking; the relief on Lily's face at the sight of him buoyed him to such an extent that he felt emboldened to act out of character. He marched up to Paluzzi's desk and said, "How dare you question my wife like she's a common criminal?"

Lily chuckled behind him, and he swung around. "Whoa, Gray. Tony and I are just having a friendly little chat. I told him about Nob and Emily."

Gray turned back to meet Paluzzi's glare.

"You should lose your job for that little piece of work, Caldwell."

"I did nothing illegal. My sister had a memento of the governor, some of his hairs for a scrapbook. We simply used those for a little test."

"An unauthorized test. On whose authority do you—"

Lily interrupted them. "On yours, Ton. Because you're going to help me now—you said so—and because if you believe me, then you believe that Stevens was the father of Emily Martin, and that he killed her, and that he killed Danny for getting too close to her, and that he'll kill me if I keep after it, especially if this little trick of his doesn't take. I assume he just wanted to get me out of the way right now, although God knows why. I'm sorry he chose your car, but that was extra clever. He puts me right back in here with you, gets you to ask all the same questions about my sanity, probably gets the whole office talking about Loony Lily again."

"Shut up, Lil," Tony said, pained.

"No. You already fired me for not shutting up, so what have I got to lose? You gonna put me in prison, Ton? Go ahead. I'll keep after him from there. I'll get Gray to do it for me. I've got two other people on my side now, too."

Tony glared at her, then rose theatrically from his seat. He pointed. "I *oughta* put you in a cell! At least I'd be able to keep tabs on you."

"You want to know where I'm going, I'll tell you. Gray and I are going to visit the address you gave us, the one for Emily's mother. I assume she'd like to know what really happened to her daughter; maybe she'll have some idea why Emily's father had to see her dead."

Tony scowled some more, but he sat back down. "You driving?"

"We'll take the train. It'll be a four-hour ride as it is."

He nodded, then cracked his knuckles loudly. "All right. I want a report from Indianapolis. We're on eggshells here, Lil, and I'm putting a whole lot of faith in your cockamamie story."

"It's sweet of you to say that," she said dryly.

"Don't fuck up."

"If you find my prints on a dead body while I'm gone," Lily said, sailing toward the door, where Gray already stood, "remember I have an alibi."

———————

Camilla Martin was making a quilt. It had been real therapy for her, immersing herself in this hobby, learning the different stitches, mastering the walking foot on her new machine, sewing the passions of her life into endless works of art. She gave the finished products to friends, to George's family, to the church bazaars. She made them for babies: sweet receiving blankets in delicate, sherbet-colored pastels. There were quilts in every room of her house. Somehow, it helped to ease the pain, better than any other hobby she'd tried, better than the therapist who had pushed too hard and caused agony, exposed her carefully repressed anguish like a raw nerve. She'd dropped the therapy. The doctor warned her that it was a "crucial" time in their sessions, but as far as she was concerned, nothing was crucial anymore. Not for years—not since Emily had died.

George had been sad, but he'd understood. George supported her always, unconditionally. Without him, she knew, she would have perished long ago, of shame or of misery or, later, of sadness. Without George, she would have been bereft. He walked into the room with his Cubs hat on and his tool belt hanging off his jeans. "Gonna fix that stair rail," he said, putting an affectionate hand on her head. "Then you won't have to worry about it wobbling right off."

"Thanks, honey," she said, turning to smile at him. "How do you like this one?"

He peered over her shoulder at the current project: a windstorm of leaves, autumnal in shades of brown, gold, orange, and maroon.

"Your stuff should be in a museum, I swear to God. You always were an artist, Cammy. Ever since you were a kid, and I saw those sketches you did—"

"All right, George." Her tone was final. They didn't discuss her youth. Even at fifty-five years old, Camilla couldn't allow herself the indulgence of looking back. The happy memories weren't worth the risk of the bad ones. Her mind had doors, and she'd learned, through an iron control, to close them. "When I finish it, I'll put it in your den. Wouldn't it look nice there, hanging on the wall?"

"You bet it would," George agreed.

Camilla sighed. "The next one I do, I think it will be a story quilt. You know, like the one they showed at my last quilter's club meeting? I want to do Emily's story. Her life in images, on a quilt. I think it would be . . . comforting. To wrap around me when I'm old."

George said nothing, but he embraced her from behind, warming her. She leaned her head against his arm. "I still dream about her, George. I still see her so clearly. Do you think somehow she comes to me that way?"

He gave it serious thought. "Is she happy in the dreams?" he asked.

"Always."

"Then I think she is. She wants you to know it's all right. There's happiness beyond. She was always such a sunshine girl, our Emily."

"Yes." The syllable held pride and pain.

"Cammy. You still have to live. Maybe she wants you to know that, too. I wish I'd given you more babies. To comfort you now."

She turned around, tears spiking her eyes. "You are my comfort. And it's not your fault I couldn't have more children."

A knock at the door surprised them both. "That's the kitchen," George said.

"I'll get it," Camilla said. "I wanted some tea, anyway."

She made her way down the hall, thoughts of Emily in her mind. She realized she was still holding a quilt square in her hand, a red leaf on a brown background. She set it down on the table and opened the door, peering through the screen. "Yes?" she asked.

The bullet pierced the screen and her chest before she had even discerned that what this visitor was holding was a gun. The impact threw her back against her table and down to the floor. While she lay there, in dwindling consciousness and growing pain, Camilla was able to determine only two things: she'd been shot, square in the heart, it seemed, and yet it wasn't the worst thing that had ever happened to her.

She turned to see another form approaching; it was George, rushing, calling her name. She reached toward him, wanting comfort, and her world went black.

Harvey sat at his desk, frowning at a report. When he looked up and saw Claudia Caldwell walking toward him on her amazingly high heels, he blinked for a moment, wondering if he was imagining her. He hadn't gotten much sleep, but he didn't think he was at the hallucination stage.

"Harvey," she said. "I have to be back at work in one hour. But I need to know, as a reporter. Something was bugging you last night, and I want to know what it was." She perched on the edge of his desk and met his gaze with a frank one of her own.

He took a moment to appreciate her: her slightly windblown blonde hair—true blonde, he knew from a picture he'd seen at Gray's house, with the two of them and a couple of brothers as kids, eating a watermelon on their front porch—her lovely, distinctive green eyes, flashing now with curiosity and something like annoyance, and her trim figure, clad in a brown wool suit belted tightly at the waist. "And you came out here to ask me that? You could have just called on the—"

"Stop. Like I said, I only have an hour. And I needed to see your face. It's very communicative, which is how I could tell you were brooding."

He stalled, wanting to flirt with her. "Maybe I was brooding about how beautiful you are."

Her chin came up. "Don't use your lines on me."

"That's not a line. What if a woman really is beautiful? What's a guy supposed to say?"

"He's supposed to say nothing, unless she's his wife or his—girlfriend or something."

"Okay, marry me."

"I'm not going to tell you again to stop it."

"Good, I'm getting tired of that." He smiled at her but didn't turn on the charm. She hated his charm, apparently.

"Harvey, please. If we're going to be a team on this . . ."

He sighed, tipping back in his chair. "I'm not so sure you and I should get involved. Sweet as Lily is, I don't know—"

Suddenly Claudia was right there, in his face, all aggression, yanking his chair legs back onto the floor. "Listen. You tell me right now what's bugging you. I didn't get my job just because I'm attractive, no matter what schmucks like you believe. I'm a reporter, and a good one, and I can see your brain through your eyes, and it's working on something. I want to know what it is."

Her closeness was distracting him, especially the appeal of her lips at this proximity. He'd been staring at her mouth for most of the speech. Now, before he thought about it, he grabbed her head in his hands and kissed her, hard, his hands sliding into her hair. She pulled away, but not immediately, and they both knew what that meant.

"Two things," he said, slightly out of breath. "One, if you stick your face in my face, I'm going to kiss you. Two, you kiss real nice." He waited, wincing slightly, for a blow, or at the very least a verbal lashing. Instead he watched the most unexpected thing happen. She blushed and went shy, like a girl on her first date. "Claudia," he began, but she held up her hand.

"Okay. I'm sorry I got in your face," she said, going back to her spot on the desk.

"I'm not," he said.

"I'm going. I didn't come here to flirt with you. You seem to think I am dying to get you into bed, but—"

"Claudia, calm down. I can't help it if I think you're pretty, and I can't help it if I want to kiss you. I'm amazed that you get angry every time I respond to you in the most natural way. But fine, you want all business, you've got it. Here's my problem, since you're so hellfire-bent on solving it."

He picked up his report and flung it into her lap. "Take a gander at that."

She looked surprised and, he hoped, a bit disappointed. "What is it?"

"It's the DNA results. The Stevens-Martin samples."

"Okay. I know I just went on and on about how smart I am, but this looks like a bunch of lines to me."

He laughed. "I like you. And not just for your body, okay?"

"Great. We can be best friends," she said. "Now what is the problem with this?"

"You're holding it upside down."

She righted it and, to her credit, blushed only slightly. "Like I said, Janusek, I only have an hour."

He sighed again, looking at all the other files stacked on his desk. A coworker walked past and stared curiously at the beautiful blonde sitting on Harvey's worktable. Harvey felt a jolt of pride. He was annoyed, too, though. He had been pulled into this whole thing against his will, and now he was stuck with it. Knowledge could be a burden.

"Okay," he said. "Let me explain."

ELEVEN

"I DON'T THINK WE should call first," Lily insisted. "We should just go, appear at their door."

"It's a long ride to make to find out they're on vacation or have suddenly moved or, all due respect to your ex-chief, he gave us the wrong address."

Lily grumbled. "You're taking away the element of surprise."

Gray nodded. "Exactly. Much more precise this way."

"Because you're a scientist." She smiled shyly at him.

"Don't get me all excited, Lily." He clutched the phone in his hand, looking half-tempted to lunge at her.

"Make the call." She sat at the kitchen table and watched him as he dug his cellular phone out of his briefcase.

Gray dialed and waited. He held up a finger. "Answering machine," he mouthed. He left a brief message, giving Lily's name and his and saying that they'd like to ask a few questions about Emily Martin. He gave their phone number, then hung up. "Sorry, baby. Just a machine. Now what? You still want to travel four hours if they might not be home? How about if we give them some time to call back? And I'll make lunch. You haven't eaten all day, have you? Those bastards came to get you, and—"

"Thanks, Gray."

He stopped, surprised. "For what?"

"For coming for me, and for standing up to Paluzzi with me. It feels so good to have someone, to have someone . . ." The tears were near again.

"Hey, toughie, you gonna get weepy on me?" Gray was in front of her in an instant, holding her face in his hands.

"God, Gray, I never used to cry, did I? I never used to." She pressed her lips together, trying to control her face.

"Crying is a necessary and cleansing action. The body needs you to cry with a certain regularity—"

Lily sniffed, amused. "Okay, Mr. Science. Thanks for the lecture. But this isn't about what my body needs. It's about how I'm not the same, how I'm not as good. Danny always used to say that I was different from the other female officers, that you couldn't depend on them not to get emotional, but he said he'd bet his life on—"

She stopped, suddenly nauseous. It was a memory that came unbidden, and it hadn't come back until now. *He'd said he would bet his life on her.* "Oh, God," she said, trying to get up, with a vague plan of running away.

Gray held her in place. "Stop it, Lily. Stop it!" He shook her. He was yelling—something Gray never did. "Stop turning him into a fucking saint! He wasn't, and it wasn't your fault he got shot. Why do you haul that guilt around with you? Why is Danny the only one who escapes your criticism?"

She stared up at him. Her eyes felt as though they were bulging out of her face. "What are you talking about? I never said Danny was a saint."

Gray's voice was bitter. "You don't have to. I hear it every day. Danny said this, and Danny said that—a reading from the holy book of Danny. Danny is watching over me while I solve this crime!" He was mimicking her voice as he quoted her words from the night before, after the dinner with Claudia and Harvey.

Lily was stunned speechless, both by his cruelty and by the unexpected attack on her idol. "He was a guy, Lily, just a guy like everyone else," Gray said, more quietly and with great weariness.

She pushed him away. "What the hell did Danny ever do to you?"

Gray shook his head. "Never mind. Let it go."

"What do you mean, let it go? You brought it up! You just lashed out like a crazy man at Danny, poor dead Danny, and I've never heard you say a word against him! What the hell is this all about?"

Gray shook his head, almost sulkily, she thought. She stood up and faced him eye to eye. "What's this all about? What's in your craw about my partner? He was a good, decent man who—"

"Wanted to sleep with you."

"What?" Lily gaped at him. "Are you out of your mind? He was my partner, my friend! He was twenty years older than I was! He never made one inappropriate gesture, never acted in any way other than— Gray, that is so low of you. I can't believe you would say this about him. Why? Why would you make such an accusation?"

Gray glared at her, his face reddening. "Have you ever looked in the mirror, Lily? You may be sublimely unaware of your attractiveness, but I guarantee no guy on earth is. I saw the way he looked at you."

She stood, hands on hips, lips parted, trying to think of some words, some way to deal with this sudden barrage of bad feelings. Her eyes scanned the kitchen as though for inspiration. They landed finally on the tile floor and stayed there. "I don't know what to say to that."

"There's nothing to say. He wanted you, and I knew you were in that car with him day after day. Maybe you wanted him, too."

"For God's sake, Gray," she said hotly, looking back at his eyes. "I married *you*. I love you. You knew that then and you know that now."

"Did you love Danny, too?"

"Of course I loved Danny! Like a father, or an older brother! I knew him before you, Gray. He was happy for me when we got engaged. He told me I'd made a great choice. He said he—"

"Yes?"

"I don't know, something like, if he had to pick someone for me that wasn't . . . him, it would be you. But he was joking. I don't even remember his exact words; it was a long time ago. He was joking."

"Fine." Gray nodded and walked to the refrigerator. "Let me get started on lunch."

Lily stared at his back, feeling somehow cheated. "That's it? You make all those accusations and then you just walk away?"

He shrugged, examining some lettuce leaves. "We just see the same thing through two different lenses, Lily. I'm sorry I got angry. Just don't expect me to buy into the greatness and untouchability of Danny Donovan. He loved you, and he wanted you, and he wasn't honest about it. He let you climb in that car every day like a lamb, not knowing what he was thinking."

"You're just making this up! You're just—weaving this reality so that you have something to be jealous about! I never would have thought that you—"

"I heard him at our wedding." His voice was quiet. He selected two bowls from a cabinet and arranged the lettuce in them.

Lily walked closer. "Heard what? What are you talking about?"

"At the reception. I walked into the men's room and heard your name, so I stayed in the little foyer there, that fancy foyer with chairs in it, like guys are going to sit and chat before they pee."

Neither of them smiled. "And?"

"And I heard someone telling him it was too bad, his pretty partner went and got herself married. And Danny said yeah, he still couldn't believe it. Stuff like that." Gray's eyes were lowered, and Lily knew he was holding back.

"What did he say, Gray?" she asked.

"I'm sorry I brought this up. You made me feel defensive, and I—"

"For God's sake, just tell me what he said." She had to know now; she needed the information.

Gray scratched his cheekbone with the back of one hand. His eyes looked past her. "He said he wished he had fucked you at least once."

Lily's head felt too heavy for her body, felt wobbly on her shoulders. "Oh."

"Lily—"

She didn't hear him. She ran away, up to her room, and closed the door softly. She lay on the bed, pillowing her heavy head. She wanted to shut her eyes; for once she wanted sleep to come. It didn't, though, and she stared at her ceiling without even blinking. Memories played like old movies in her mind, but somehow they were wrong, they were poorly dubbed, and she couldn't trust their veracity.

She tried to hear Danny's voice, the voice that was always with her like a conscience or a guide. She tried to summon it, to make it address Gray's accusations. All she heard were the distant sounds of her husband in the kitchen, chopping things and opening and closing cabinets. She couldn't hear Danny at all, her Danny, oh Danny Boy. She had sung that to him as a joke, lots of times. Her voice was fair, but she'd always started too high on purpose so that she'd be squeaking out the refrain in a way guaranteed to make him laugh until he wiped at his eyes.

Now, alone in her room, she seemed to smell nail varnish, strong and pungent and cruel. She couldn't picture Danny, but she had a sudden vivid image of Fred, pushing her down, telling her she was pretty. "Make sure you don't talk about what happened between us," she heard him saying again in his careless way. He'd implied her complicity, had practically winked at her. He probably even believed, from his own twisted perspective, that she had wanted him.

What she'd wanted was her father. She'd wanted him to come back from the dead and kill Fred. She wanted her father now, too. Perhaps he was the only man who could tell her the truth about other men, about the things they said and did, about the pain they inflicted with their words and their hands. Or, in extreme cases, with guns.

———————

She was back in the street, smelling the rain, feeling the concrete hard under her back. He stood above her, laughing, and this time Danny was laughing, too, even as he died. She lifted her legs and kicked out, hitting her assailant in the kneecaps. He crumpled soundlessly, his face distorted, growing larger like a balloon. As his head grew, his body diminished, until there was almost nothing there for Lily to attack, but she threw her punches anyway, hitting him in soft spots, vulnerable places. He gave no more resistance than the academy dummy, and she felt fury and frustration. "Fight me!" she screamed. "Fight back, dammit!"

Nothing happened; when she looked at the ground, barely anything was left. Just bits of clothing and flesh. When Lily held up her hands, they were covered with blood.

The phone rang, waking her. Lily picked it up quickly, before Gray could get the downstairs extension. "Hello?" she said.

"Is this Lily Caldwell?" the quavering voice said.

"Yes. I'm Lily. Who is this?"

There was a pause and something like a gasp. "My name is George Martin. You called looking for my wife."

"Yes, Mr. Martin. I wondered if I could talk to her. We'd like to come out—"

111

"My wife is in the hospital, Mrs. Caldwell, in intensive care. She was shot today. Through the door of our own home. I'm just here to get a few clothes, and then I'm going back to be with—"

"What's her prognosis?" Lily asked. "Is she going to be all right?"

The man on the other end began to cry. "I don't know," he wailed. "They shot her, right in the chest. Can you imagine?"

Yes, I can imagine, Lily thought.

"My wife is fifty-five years old, with not an enemy in the world!"

But she does have an enemy.

"Did they catch her assailant?" Lily asked.

"No. When I got there, he was gone. Just came to the door, shot her, and took off. Some neighbors got a look. Said he was a thug-looking guy, maybe darker skin, something in between black and white. That's all we have." He was getting too upset to talk.

Lily felt horror; it had been lingering from her dream, but now a reality had perpetuated it. "Mr. Martin, I'm going to be praying for your wife. I'm sending positive feelings out there, and I hope she's going to be okay. And when things look better, I want to talk to you both, because I might know why she was shot."

There was a long silence. "This is about Emily, isn't it?" he asked.

"Yes, sir," she said, "I think it is."

———

She called Tony immediately afterward.

"What?" Tony asked irritably. "I thought you were going to Indy."

"Mrs. Martin was shot this morning. Shot in the chest." Lily fingered her own scar.

"How do you know?"

"Mr. Martin just returned my call. His wife is in intensive care."

"Get off the line, Lil. I gotta make some calls."

112

Lily hung up grimly. She felt terrible about Mrs. Martin, and she felt that Tony could have prevented it—they all could have—if he had listened to Lily months before. Now Nob Stevens was running scared.

Gray came into the room with a sandwich on a plate. "Will you eat?" he asked gently. "Or are you too mad at me?"

She held out her hand. He came to the bed and sat down on it. "I'm sorry I brought up all that—"

"I've been thinking about it, and I probably did have a really innocent view of Danny." She took the plate he offered and set it on her lap. Then she met his eyes. "It wasn't hurting me to have it, Gray—"

"Lily," he said, remorseful.

"—but it was obviously hurting you, so I guess it's best that we had the discussion." She moved the plate again, setting it on the table beside the bed. "I was tired, too. I haven't been sleeping well."

He nodded. Lily still wouldn't discuss the nightmares. She sighed now, rubbing her eyes and then looking into his. "I don't want to be your enemy, Gray."

He obviously went with the instinct he always had around Lily: touching her. He pulled her into his arms and kissed her, not gently. His lips traveled over her face, familiarly, and his hands twined in her hair. "I'm sorry. I have to admit, no one ever made me as jealous as he did. There was just something about him. But I wasn't lying, Lily. I wouldn't stoop to that just to destroy his image in your mind. I'm not that mean-spirited."

"You don't have a mean bone in your body. Well, maybe one or two," she said with a crooked smile, smoothing his eyebrows with both thumbs. She put out her mouth to be kissed, and Gray met her need quickly, warming her lips with his. "You taste like salami," she said. "It's making me hungry."

He pulled away, grinned, and retrieved her sandwich. "Eat. I've got a salad for you downstairs."

She took a bite and considered him. "You were on the extension. You heard about Mrs. Martin?"

Gray lowered his head. "I'd make a terrible spy. And yes, I heard. And you called Tony."

"Yeah. He bumped me off the phone to make some calls of his own."

"You're in a rat's nest, Lily."

"You're in it with me, Tonto."

"Finish your sandwich."

"Why?"

He reached out to touch her red flannel shirt; he toyed with the top button, and Lily felt a pang of desire. "Because I want to have makeup sex."

"Hmm." She didn't object when he kept working at the buttons, but she didn't stop eating, either. "You know," she reflected with her mouth full, "Nob Stevens just can't seem to kill properly. The only person he succeeded with was Emily. I mean, he killed Danny, but I was supposed to die then, too. What do you think he did with Emily? Throw a flaming torch into her car? Knocking her unconscious first, of course?"

"How can you eat when you talk about that?" he asked, fingering her bra.

"I'm hungry."

"Me, too."

Lily was finished chewing. She pondered him with sleepy eyes. "I'm practicing forgiveness, Gray. I don't think I'm very good at it." She reached toward him, touching only the hem of his shirt.

Impatiently, he pulled the shirt over his head. "This would be a step in the right direction," he said, grinning at her.

She jumped up, taking another bite of her sandwich. "Just let me check my e-mail."

"Oh, Lily," he groaned, staying where he was.

She was bent over the computer. "Just a sec. There's probably nothing." She typed in her password and waited, stealing a glance at Gray's handsome physique. "Nice pecs, by the way. Okay, here it is: three messages. I can get Viagra online; did you know that, Gray?"

He snorted. "Not a necessity, as you'd see if you came over here."

"Okay, we can delete that one. We're also being offered a lower interest rate on our mortgage—oh my God! Gray, this is from Dr. Worthington!"

He was at her side in a moment. "Let's see."

She clicked her mouse and a letter appeared.

Dear Mrs. Caldwell:

I received your request about Emily Martin. I've consulted my file to refresh my memory, but as a matter of fact I recall much without aid of my files. I can tell you some basic information. I was practising in the States then, and Emily's mother, Camilla, was my patient. I delivered Emily without any complications, on 15 February 1964. Camilla was very young and frightened, but her boyfriend was present, and he seemed to be a good young man. I understood they planned to marry shortly. I am distressed to hear of Emily's death. It is especially unfortunate, because, without going into any great detail, I can assure you that she and her mother had already suffered much in their lives.

There is not much more I can say without breaching my client's confidentiality. If you have further questions that you feel I can answer, do call me.

Sincerely,
Ian Worthington

He left his phone exchange. Lily read the letter twice, then looked at Gray. "Does that tell us anything?"

Gray shrugged. "He seems to acknowledge a secret having to do with the Martins. So that's . . . something."

"Yeah," Lily said uncertainly, staring at the computer.

Gray took her hand, then looked at it more closely. "Lily, where's your wedding ring?" He looked at his own left hand. "I never took mine off. I kept hoping."

Her head flew up; her startled eyes met his. "I didn't think—"

The doorbell rang. Lily's eyes widened. "The mailman?"

Gray shook his head. "It's past time for the mail." He consulted his watch. "It's already four o'clock. I'll get it. And then we'll talk about your ring, okay?" He grabbed his shirt and began to put it back on as he walked out of the room.

Lily sighed; she really hadn't thought about her ring since Gray had come back. After all, they'd been distracted with all of the Emily Martin business. She hadn't been certain of what would happen between Gray and her, although now she was. She hadn't meant to keep the ring off as any sort of statement. She just hadn't thought of it. Had she? She hovered near the computer, wondering if she should contact Ian Worthington again. Gray's voice came to her distinctly from the bottom of the stairs. It sounded urgent, even anxious. "Lily, you need to come down here."

She buttoned her shirt and descended quickly, finding Gray by the door with a man she'd never seen before. He was young, trim, nondescript. Fair hair and glasses. "Hello," she said uncertainly.

"Hello," he said. He looked half-ready to run away.

Lily turned to Gray. "What's going on?"

The visitor answered her. "As I told your husband, my name is John Pierre. I work for Governor Stevens."

116

Lily's faintness was so sudden she didn't initially realize why Gray was gripping her around the waist. She heard Gray say, "What are you doing here?"

The man named Pierre pushed up the sleeves of his Oxford shirt—nervously, Lily thought. "I'd be fired if he knew I was here. I'll be fired anyway." He looked miserable but somehow determined. "I decided today that I had to find out some things for myself. I need to hear your side of the story."

"What story?" asked Lily carefully.

"I've had you watched for months; the governor feared you would hurt his campaign. He told me that you were ill, that you were delusional. But now that his wife is missing—"

"Linda Stevens?"

"Yes, ma'am," Pierre said politely. "And his behavior has been such that I—I'm questioning everything, and I don't know what to think, and I felt I needed to start with you. I'm out on a limb here, so I hope this can remain confidential."

Gray was still holding Lily's waist. "I think we'd better sit down," he said. "Can I offer you some coffee?"

Lily noted Pierre's stiffness as he accompanied her into their living room; Gray went to the kitchen. Lily didn't know what to say. This man had worked for the governor, watched her for him. Now was her chance: what did she want to know? She was trying to formulate a question when Pierre pointed at her mail table. "That's from Governor Stevens."

"What?"

"That letter. That's his stationery and his handwriting."

Lily went to the table and picked up the cream-colored envelope, almost as thick as a wedding invitation and, she noted grimly as she tore it open, lined with elegant gold paper.

"What is it?" asked Pierre urgently.

Lily would have said, "None of your business" if she hadn't been staring so fixedly at the note in her hand. *Dear Lily Caldwell*, it began, scrawled in bold black that made Lily think of spiders.

> *I have long admired your accomplishments as a Capitol City police officer, most especially your dignity after your shooting and the unfortunate death of your partner, Officer Donovan. I'd like to meet with you, one on one, to discuss your future in the force. Please make an appointment with my secretary tomorrow so that we can discuss my recommendation that you be reinstated on the CCPD and promoted for your acts of valor.*
>
> *With sincere admiration,*
> *Robert Stevens*

Gray had entered the room, and Lily wordlessly handed him the letter, narrowing her eyes to study Pierre. "There's no stamp on that letter. Did you bring it?"

Pierre looked surprised. "No, ma'am. Is it from the—"

"I can't believe he would have come here himself, and yet I'm starting to think he would," she said thoughtfully. She looked at Gray, who was frowning at the note.

"He's bribing you," he said. "He's offering you compensation for letting it go."

Pierre looked impatient. "Please, may I ask—"

Gray handed him the letter hesitantly. Pierre read it, and Gray and Lily regarded him mistrustfully. Pierre shook his head while his eyes scanned the words. "This doesn't make sense. He doesn't write letters like this. He doesn't make personal contacts, not unless it's part of the campaign PR. And he doesn't admire you, he thinks you're crazy."

"And maybe he sent you here to have that reaction, so that we'd be confused and uncertain," Lily said.

Pierre frowned. "Mrs. Caldwell, I'm concerned about Linda Stevens. Somehow she slipped past the governor's security men and left without telling him her destination. From what I understand from the night guard, Mrs. Stevens made up a story to get out, and now the governor is uncertain of her whereabouts. This is very unlike her. I thought she was relatively happy with him, but this—it's so unusual, on top of the way he's been acting regarding you—"

"And how is that?" Lily asked.

"Nervous. Obsessive. He wanted daily reports, minute details. At the time I thought it was because he considered you crazy, but now I think he feels threatened by you for other reasons."

"Why did he consider me crazy? You keep saying that."

"He heard about your suspicion that he shot you and, uh, your partner."

"How?" Lily asked, feeling suddenly numb.

"Someone on the force. Word had gotten around. When the governor heard, he told me to watch you, told me that your lies could threaten his campaign."

"They're not lies," Lily said. She stared at Pierre. He looked away first. "So why do you think he wants to see me?" she asked.

"I have no idea. If he is trying to bribe you, well, I suppose that's why."

"He doesn't know Lily very well," Gray said, "or he wouldn't have tried this."

"He doesn't know me at all," Lily said. "But he will tomorrow."

Gray put his hands on his hips. "You're not going?"

"Oh yes, I am," Lily said, energized by the thought. "The more I think about it, the more I'm looking forward to it. Finally looking Nob Stevens in the eye. Saying what I've wanted to say for a year."

119

Pierre put out a hand. "I can't advise it, Mrs. Caldwell."

Lily flashed a smile at him. "Sit down, Mr. Pierre. I want to ask you some things about your boss."

TWELVE

"WHAT ARE WE GOING to do?" asked Claudia, back in Harvey's office. Most of the regular staff had gone, but she and he had met again to discuss his findings and determine their course of action. "We can't leave this alone." Her brows were creased in an almost disbelieving frown.

Harvey shrugged. "Sure we can."

She stared at him. "This is dynamite, Harvey. It affects everything. It's important to Lily's cause, to her life, to her happiness. And it's important that we expose the governor—"

"See, that's the part I'm not so eager about. I have a career to think of, and this test was done without his permission. It's probably not even admissible in court. I don't want to be the slimy scientist who—"

"You are who you are. You don't have to accept any labels. And now that you know this, you have an obligation." Her eyes glowed with intensity. She sat in a chair pulled close to his, and they spoke in low tones.

He leaned his head back on his chair and closed his eyes. "Lily's not going to let this go, and you sure as hell aren't. I'm trapped by women on crusades." He opened one eye. "Can I at least ask for a reward if I stick my neck out?"

She sat straighter in her chair, all dignity. "What kind of reward?"

"Dinner? Just you and me?"

"Is that all?" she asked carefully.

"Should I ask for more?"

"No."

He laughed. "Okay, that's all. A nice dinner somewhere elegant. Music, tablecloths, real silverware. A few hours of your time and company."

"Harvey, you have a deal."

She put out her hand, and he shook it with a wry smile. "Can't we seal the bargain with a kiss?"

To his great surprise, she leaned in and touched her lips softly to his. It shocked his system far more than such a little kiss should have. "Now let's get to Grayson's house before you change your mind," she said. She walked toward the door without looking back.

———

Nob Stevens had always been able to control his anger, to convert it into useable energy. The fact that Pierre hadn't called back was a thorn in Nob's side, and he called the Randall secretary himself, muting his voice slightly.

"Josh Randall Studio," she said brightly.

"Hello! My name is David Harris. I was in talks with Josh Randall about a piece I wanted to give my wife on our wedding day. We were supposed to meet again this week, and—"

"Really? I don't see anything in the calendar here, Mr. Harris."

Bitch, Nob thought, glaring out of the tinted windows of his limo. He was headed toward a meeting that would be very stressful, and he needed some closure on these unresolved issues. "No, we'd spoken by phone, but our arrangements were sort of vague. Anyway, I'd sent a friend of mine to make an appointment. I think he came in today—"

"Oh, was that Mr. Langdon?"

"Yes, that's my friend." Nob and Pierre had agreed on the story and the aliases beforehand. Nob took a certain pleasure—almost a childish delight—in the occasional subterfuge. "I wonder, because I'm on the road and I haven't heard from him—did you indicate where I might find Josh Randall?"

"I told Mr. Langdon the same as I'll tell you: this was an unexpected leave of absence, very unexpected. I was frankly shocked when Josh called me, so there's not a lot I can tell his customers, except to keep in touch. Josh will be calling in for his messages, so—"

"But is there another studio he might be visiting? I'm on the road, so I could go to see him there."

"He didn't give me any info, so that means he doesn't want people to contact him. He has various other properties, but I don't know where they are or what—"

"Other properties? You mean that he owns?" Nob tried to sound impressed.

"Oh, sure. He has another home besides the one here in Capitol City, sort of a vacation home, and I know he has an uncle with a cabin somewhere, and he visits there, too. So anyway, I can't put you in touch with him until he calls in. I'm sorry about that, Mr. Harris. As soon as Josh returns, I'll be happy to pencil you in on the calendar."

"That would be great." Nob made some silly chitchat, not even thinking about what his mouth was saying, and then he clicked off.

He stared at the streets of Capitol City, mysterious in dusk, holding the promise of power, of the future. Pierre had not checked in. What was holding him up? The boy had been reliable, always. What was it that prevented him from sharing that news about the vacation home and the cabin? Nob had ways of finding those addresses; he could have had them by now, and he could be on his way to Linda, on his way to silencing her. He swore under his breath.

He dialed his phone again, gave some brief instructions to his secretary, and then rang off. He was almost at city hall; the meeting with the mayor was a crucial one, and he couldn't call it off, even for his growing personal problems.

He pulled at his impeccable tie and mussed his hair. He would stop at the water fountain before he entered the mayor's office to make sure his hand was cold and clammy when the other man clasped it.

The meeting had to be faced, but there was no saying he couldn't leave early.

Nob grinned to himself. He felt a touch of the flu coming on.

Pierre called in just as Nob was leaving city hall, about half an hour later. "Where the hell have you been?" Stevens barked.

"I'm so sorry, sir. I had just interviewed the secretary when I had the bad luck to run into an old girlfriend. She was very persistent, making a scene, and I—"

Stevens grunted. "What did you find out?" It was a test, and Pierre knew it. In all likelihood Stevens had already gleaned the information. He wasn't a man who waited for phone calls.

"The artist has two possible hiding places: there's a vacation home and a cabin owned by his uncle. If we can find out the addresses, sir, I can drive out tonight."

"That won't be necessary," said Stevens smoothly. "I'll need to talk to Linda myself. Clear the air. Della is getting the addresses as we speak." There was a pause. "Don't let me down again, Pierre. I expect you tomorrow, early."

"Yes, sir. And I won't, sir."

Pierre clicked off his phone and turned to the Caldwells. "He's going to find his wife tonight."

"He's going to kill her," Lily said. "If she knows anything, he's going to kill her."

Gray looked at Lily in disbelief, then helplessly at Pierre. "We need to call there. We need to find the phone numbers. You're his right-hand man; can't you call in a favor from someone? Someone the governor won't have already talked to?"

Pierre shook his head. "I don't know. I can't make him suspicious, and if word gets back to him—wait. There is someone. If she's still at the office, she can use her computer. The governor doesn't even deal with her; she's just someone—that I see sometimes."

He knew he was blushing, and he felt a certain shame. His entire persona as the governor's man was falling apart. He was a double agent, with no more sophistication than a schoolboy. Still, his conscience wasn't troubling him anymore.

"Let me call her," he said.

Twenty minutes later Pierre had the addresses and phone numbers he needed. He handed them to Gray and Lily. "You can do the honors," he said. "I wouldn't even know what to say."

Gray was halfway to the phone when they saw lights in their drive-way. "Oh, God," Lily said nervously. "Tell me that's not him." She ran to the window and looked out. She felt a shock when she saw not one, but two cars. Claudia emerged from the first one, and Lily's heart calmed slightly. In a moment she saw three people convening in the darkness: Claudia, Harvey, and Tony Paluzzi.

"Chief Paluzzi," said Claudia, extending her hand. "I don't know if you remember me, but I'm—"

"I know who you are," Tony said, trying to push past her. "I gotta talk to Lily."

"So do we," said Claudia quietly. Something in her tone alerted him. Paluzzi turned, mouth gaping, and saw her tense expression, saw the man who held up an envelope like a talisman. "Who the hell are you?" he asked, looking at Harvey.

"Harvey Janusek. I work in the Exeter Lab, in Brompton. Gray had me do a DNA analysis of—"

"Don't even tell me," Paluzzi yelled. "Goddammit." He huffed his way to the door, angry and fearful. "They're breaking laws left and right, I'm guessing." The three of them waited as Paluzzi rang the doorbell.

Claudia studied Paluzzi curiously, and he finally met her stare with one of his own. "I think we can all conclude that we are in some very deep crap here," he muttered.

Harvey nodded, with feeling, and held up his envelope. "I'm afraid this makes it deeper."

THIRTEEN

LINDA PICKED AT THE salad Josh had made her. He himself had eaten heartier fare, but she'd wanted nothing at all, then at his insistence had asked for greens. Josh had been solicitous, concerned. Unlike Nob, he wanted to talk to her, wanted to work things out, and for the first time since her marriage Linda felt reluctant to do so. First, she didn't want to involve Josh any more than she had to. Second, she'd avoided looking at the information head-on, avoided considering all of its implications, and to talk it out meant she would have to think.

She smiled weakly at Josh as he sat next to her at the table. "I appreciate this, all of it," she said, pushing her plate away and clutching his arm.

He shook his head. "Linda, you're grateful. I get that. Do you think I need to hear it more than once? Don't you think I'm happy just to be alone with you? I never got over you, you know."

"Oh, Josh—"

"I may as well say it. There's a lot more I should have said, years ago, and then maybe I'd have had more of a chance with you."

Linda looked into his face, a face she'd once loved dearly. "Josh. I've been thinking of you so much lately, you wouldn't believe me."

"Things haven't been good with him, have they?"

"No," she said, looking away. "Even before last night—no, they weren't good. I think I sedated myself emotionally. I never asked myself if I was happy, but I knew I wasn't. It's not just about my marriage, though, Josh. I found something out—something about Nob. It's hard to believe, and yet I do believe it now, and I don't think I should tell you. Somehow I think I'd be putting you in danger."

Josh pulled her toward him and slid his arms around her like a protective belt. "You need to tell someone. Tell me. I'm not afraid of Nob Stevens. I never have been. Except the day I found out that he won and I lost. But that wasn't fear, that was hate."

"Oh, Josh." She buried her face in his shoulder.

"Linda, when all this is over, when we resolve it somehow—are you going to go back to him?"

She shuddered; he felt it like a spasm against his skin. "Never. I can't believe I lived with him. I can't believe I let him touch me!"

Her tone raised the hairs on his arms. "Linda, what the hell is going on here?"

The phone rang, and she jumped. "Who has this number?" she said.

"Well, my uncle, for one. Calm down. How could Nob possibly know where we are?" he asked calmly, striding to the kitchen wall phone. He picked it up. "Hello?"

"Mr. Randall?" It was a woman's voice. A young woman's, to judge by its timbre.

"Yes. Who is this?"

"My name is Lily Caldwell. I was a police officer in Capitol City. I don't know if you remember my name; it was in the papers. My partner was shot and killed a year ago, and I was shot and—"

Josh felt a sense of disconnectedness. The world that made sense had faded, and he was in limbo with a woman he loved but somehow couldn't have, and now a woman he'd never met was calling him on this phone in the middle of the forest . . .

"I know who you are," he interrupted. "Why exactly are you calling me, and how did you get this number?"

He heard despair in her voice. She obviously feared he'd hang up, which he was on the verge of doing. "I've worked for the last year to try to find evidence that the governor shot my partner and me."

"What?" Josh asked, his eyes darting to Linda.

"I still believe it firmly, but I found out today, through a man in the governor's office, that his wife is missing, possibly with you. Please believe me when I tell you I think she is in danger. Please also believe that he knows where you are and that if I'm right he'll be arriving there as fast as his car can take him."

"This is—I can't take this in," Josh said, raking a hand through his long hair.

Linda ran to him and touched his arm. "What is it? Who is it?" she whispered.

"Miss Caldwell, why do you think—"

"God, please don't stay on the line with me. Just get out of there. I don't want him to kill anyone else, do you understand? I feel enough guilt about my partner. Run now, ask questions later. You can look me up in Capitol City. You can call me when you get to another location. But don't go to your other house. He knows about that, too."

"How do—"

"Just go!" she cried, and Josh saw the lights of a car turning into the driveway.

He slammed down the phone. "Grab your purse and your bag. Out the back door, now!"

In twenty seconds they were behind the cabin and fleeing through the dark woods, tripping over stumps and roots that they couldn't see, running with an eerie silence in which even breathing seemed deathly loud. Josh kept his ears attuned to the action behind him. He heard a car door slam; a minute later he heard something like glass breaking. They hadn't taken the time to turn out the lights, and Linda's salad still sat on the table. Their visitor would know, instantly, that they had run. How determined would he be to come after them?

Josh thought fast. If Stevens came into the woods, he would be a few minutes behind them. They could keep running, but it would be exhausting, and Linda obviously couldn't do it all night. He wished he had a compass; there was a little shelter, a fisherman's hut, that he and Linda could stay in until he arranged for their escape somewhere else, but he'd only found it once while hiking, and that had been in the bright light of day.

They paused and leaned against a tree. "Do you have your cell phone in your purse?" he whispered into her ear.

"Yes."

"We'll find a place I know, then we'll call for reinforcements." His voice was barely louder than a sigh, but Linda nodded.

She followed him without question, without complaint. He'd always admired Linda's lack of frilliness, especially considering her former profession. She was elegant but practical. She held his hand without clinging, and her long legs kept stride with his as they developed a rhythm and changed course, heading toward what he hoped was shelter. If worse came to worst, he thought, they'd have to sleep in the open, and in the morning he'd figure out where they were. Or they could approach one of the other vacation homes and ask for shelter until a ride came. Someone might recognize Linda, though, and that might not be good . . .

She slid closer to him and put her mouth near his ear. "I'm sorry, Josh," she said.

He stopped and wrapped his arms around her. "I love you, Linda. I always have."

He peered at her in the dark. He could see a glistening in her eyes; he wondered if it was a sheen of tears. She leaned forward and kissed him softly, on the lips, then held his hand again. She nodded, and they walked on. None of their conversation had been louder than the gentle sounds of the forest around them.

———————

Nob sat in the cabin, thinking. He'd helped himself to a beer from the refrigerator. A glance at the woods, as well as a brief description of the area from a helpful citizen at the rest area, convinced him that they would have to return. Their things were here; maybe if they didn't see his car, which he had already taken the liberty of hiding down the road, they would feel emboldened to return. He couldn't wait all night, but he could have someone ready.

He dialed his phone; Pierre answered on the second ring.

"Sir?" he said. "Were you able to—"

"Quiet. I need you down here. It may take longer than I thought; they bolted when I got here." He paused. "Are you there?"

"Yes, sir."

"You'll have to drive down. I'll give you directions, and—"

"Sir, I didn't want to bother you with this, but I won't be able to come."

"What?" Nob was losing patience. This growing chaos, this entropy, was disorienting him, affecting his confidence. "Why the hell not? I told you, Pierre, not to let me down again."

"It's just that I've been detained, sir. By the police."

"What? What the fuck is going on?"

"I don't know, sir. I was asked to come to the police station. The chief of Homicide, Chief Paluzzi, said he wanted to speak with me. I'm here waiting to be interviewed."

"Shit," Nob said, almost calmly. "Shit, this had better not be about me."

"How could it be, sir?" asked Pierre, his voice sounding strange, unfamiliar.

"Because of that bitch Lily Caldwell. Paluzzi was her superior officer. She probably bent his ear and cried her pretty eyes out, and now he's nosing around my office."

"He didn't say, sir."

"Obviously you'll say nothing about Lily Caldwell."

"Well, if they ask me, sir, I'll simply say that Miss Caldwell is disturbed, that she's a threat to your—"

"Say nothing. You didn't follow her; you don't know her."

"But, sir, you're in the right here. You're the governor of the state. I don't think—"

"Good. You're not paid to think. And you're paid very well, Pierre."

"Yes, sir."

"Call me the second they're done with you."

"Yes, sir."

Nob hung up; he squeezed the phone so hard he felt the cheap plastic crack under his hand. "Things have changed," he muttered. "It's time for the big guns."

He dialed again, a number he knew by heart on the off chance that he'd ever have to use it.

John Pierre faced the room of tense people. "They got away."

He heard Lily's relieved exhalation and understood her emotion. He'd been feeling it himself. "He's hanging around the cottage, thinking they'll return. He wanted me to come with him, to help hunt for them, just like Chief Paluzzi said he would."

He sent a respectful glance toward Paluzzi, and Paluzzi eyed him speculatively. "That wouldn't have been safe for you, son, not if he got wind of this little meeting. He's not a stupid man."

"No, sir." Pierre took his tape recorder out of his pocket and tossed it to Paluzzi. "That's everything I've done for him in recent days. I record my actions as a form of organization. I'm resigning as of now, and I'll leave that tape and some others to you, if they can be of any help. If *I* can be of any help." He squinted apologetically at Lily.

Harvey stood up and jingled some change in his pocket. "What do we do now? Can't you arrest him?"

Paluzzi sighed. "Not with the evidence in that envelope, not the way it was obtained. But good Lord, that's some powerful stuff. And what other evidence have we got? Lily's dream? I'm sorry, Lil, you know I believe you now, but that's still not going to wash with anyone else."

"What about Camilla Martin? Have they caught the guy who shot her? He could link it all to Stevens," Lily said hesitantly.

"No arrest yet. We don't even know if Mrs. Martin will live to talk. What we need even more is to catch him red-handed trying to cover this up. It's all he can do now to cover his mess. We don't want him to kill anyone, but we might want him to try."

"It doesn't need to come to that," Claudia said tentatively. "If we leaked this to the press"—she held up her hand at the immediate protests all around her—"they would do their own investigation. It would be rapid, and they'd have the information we have inside of a week. They'd reinvestigate Emily Martin; they'd find out about the missing files. That alone would kill his candidacy, and they'd be working on getting him indicted."

Paluzzi nodded. "Probably so. Probably. But it's chancy. We don't want to get sloppy now, especially if that would make him desperate."

John Pierre spoke again. "There's something you haven't considered." He was surprised to find all eyes on him, assessing him. "Uh, it's his wife. Whatever made her run. She might have evidence, too—evidence we don't know about."

There was a momentary silence. Lily broke it first. "You're right. We need to talk with Linda Stevens. We need to find those two and tell them everything and ask if they'll cooperate with us. As it is, all we can hope right now is that they're not somehow walking into Nob Stevens's web."

"So, we should . . . ?" Harvey asked.

"We should wait," Lily said. "I'm going to order a pizza."

FOURTEEN

JOSH HAD TOLD HER he feared he would take them in the wrong direction, but his inner compass was better than he knew. They found the hut an hour later and crept inside. It was cold within, and damp, but there was a small cot, and they huddled on it gratefully, pulling a musty blanket around them. "He won't find us here in the dark, and in the morning we'll be gone," he said.

"All right," Linda agreed, leaning on his shoulder.

"Linda. You need to tell me now. Tell me why this ex-cop I don't know is calling me and warning me that the governor might be chasing me."

Linda stared at his silhouette. "What? Is that what she said? I have no idea what that's about."

"Have you ever heard of Lily Caldwell?"

Linda shrugged. "It sounds familiar."

"She's the police officer who was shot last year in an ambush—"

"Oh yes, I remember. That was tragic. I remember her picture. She was a pretty girl. She could have been a model."

"You would know," he said softly.

He stroked her hair, and she felt peaceful. Ironically, she felt more at ease in this darkened building than she had at home with Nob. She enjoyed his warmth for a moment longer, then sat up straighter. "Josh, there's something I have to tell you. You might not want to be involved with me afterward."

"Impossible," he said, squeezing her.

"It's about Nob. I found something yesterday. Pictures of a woman, a naked woman, and a letter from her. He had them in the pocket of his suit coat, the one he'd worn the day before."

"That doesn't seem so—"

"Josh." She leaned toward him; her lips found his ear in the dark. She whispered the truth—the truth she hadn't wanted to acknowledge.

"Good God," he said. Even in the dark she saw the disbelief on his face.

Later, after they'd talked it out, he picked up Linda's phone and called information. He found a listing for Lily Caldwell and dialed, knowing that it was late.

She answered on the second ring. "Lily Caldwell?" he asked.

"Mr. Randall?" Her voice was breathless, relieved.

"We have to talk."

"Yes, sir, we do. Do you need someone to come and get you?"

Nob began the drive home. He had a man in place at the cabin. It would be expensive, but it was worth the risk, he supposed. Linda would be taken care of; Lily would soon be taken care of. Hopefully Pierre wouldn't spill anything to the police. He would soon have it all contained.

Ironically, he felt happy as he rode through the dark streets. It was cold, and he wore only a sweater, but the heater in his luxurious car

136

was working, and he was listening to jazz on the radio, something he rarely had time to do. He thrived on conflict, and something about these loose ends brought him pleasure, just as resistance to his authority always had.

Camilla's resistance had been the first. Nob's power had been born from that. Her helplessness, her sweet vulnerability, had made him aware of his own control, his ability to command. He still loved to think about her as she was then, soft and sweet, naked, saying, "Stop, Bobby. Please stop. You mustn't do this anymore." He had laughed, his hands traveling over her, establishing his mastery. His power flowed more strongly with the flowing of her tears.

"I'll tell," she'd dared to say once, in the beginning.

"No, Cammy," he had said. His tone was enough to send her cringing away from him, but he leaned over and spoke very distinctly. "You will not tell. *You will never tell.*" And she never had.

———————

They convened Friday morning for breakfast at the Caldwell home: Lily, Gray, Paluzzi, Pierre, Harvey, and Claudia. "What's the plan?" Harvey asked. "I need to get to work."

"Me, too," Claudia said. "But I'll take the day off if it means getting the story. I assume you're going to let me scoop the world on this, right, Lily?"

Lily shrugged. "I don't see why not. You and Harvey have found our motive. We just need Linda Stevens to verify it, and we'll be off and running. I still think I should wear a wire at my meeting."

Paluzzi shook his head. "I'm not sure I like this. I'm not sure—"

"I'm sure, Tony." Lily touched his hand. "It's going to end soon. Maybe it will end today."

"What does he have to gain from meeting with you? His bribe won't pay off. What does he plan to do then?" Paluzzi asked, talking to himself.

John Pierre cleared his throat. "I have to agree with Chief Paluzzi. The governor is very determined, and he's powerful. You may have evidence, but he's going to have you on his turf. He's a clever man, and I think—I think he enjoys this, in a way. Like a game." He looked in Lily's eyes. "He doesn't intend to lose the game, Mrs. Caldwell."

"Yeah, neither did Nixon," Claudia said, sawing off a piece of her melon.

Pierre smiled thinly. "And he's very similar to Nixon, I think. He may have illusions of untouchability, but he can do some damage before you take him down."

Gray took Lily's hand. "Lily, I know you've waited a year for this. I know Tony and I both let you down, and you want your moment of vindication. But please, please, just let me go with you. I'll sit quietly; I won't get in your way. I'll be an insurance policy against any . . . anything," he finished uncertainly.

Lily squeezed the fingers that held her. "All right."

Gray's surprised expression made her laugh. "That's it? 'All right'? You're not going to fight me, tell me how tough you are, how—"

"I'm not an idiot, Gray. It's always good to have backup." She took a strawberry from the fruit tray she and Gray had assembled that morning and popped it into her mouth. She'd obviously never felt more vital, more positive. To Gray she had never looked more beautiful.

Paluzzi cleared his throat. "I got a plainclothesman on the lookout for Mrs. Stevens and her boyfriend. They should have rendezvoused by now; they were going to meet near some general store, some old-fashioned place up by all those cabins." He looked at his watch. "I'm waiting for a call, but I haven't heard anything."

"How will Linda Stevens know to trust him? How will she know it's not one of Stevens's plants?" Lily asked worriedly.

Paluzzi shrugged. "Not a problem. First of all, my plainclothesman's a she. Carol Shepard. And I told Mrs. Stevens that Carol has that bright red hair and that she would show them her police ID."

———

Linda and Josh emerged from a shelter of trees behind the store. The place looked like a big log cabin. "I'm starving," Linda confessed quietly. "Might they have anything to eat in there?" She clutched her sweater around her in the brisk air and realized that she hadn't worn clothing this casual—jeans, T-shirt, and cardigan—since before Nob was elected.

"Sure," Josh said. "Will you be all right if I—"

Linda nodded, then shook her head. "No, never mind. It's not a good idea. He said not to separate. And Josh—I think that's her."

She pointed to a white Chevy sitting in the parking lot, its hood up. A woman with flame-colored hair was peeking at something in its depths. Aside from her, only a few locals were visible: a man with a cup of coffee, just emerging from the store and looking half-asleep; a woman and two teenagers, holding fishing poles and wearing thick flannel shirts, climbing the steps to the store; and an old man who sat on the steps, reading the newspaper outdoors despite the cold.

"Let's go," Josh said.

They approached her car. Linda kept her head down, fearing that someone would recognize her. She had changed her hair, and she was letting it hang into her face, something she never normally did. She clutched Josh's hand as he said, "Having car trouble?"

The woman looked at them, her gaze sharp and assessing. "Yes, sir, but I think I've fixed it now. Can I give you two a ride into town?"

"We'd appreciate that," Josh said in a friendly tone, aiming for pleasant surprise. "We were hiking, and my wife got all tired out."

Before Linda knew it they were bundled into the Chevy. It had been backed into its space. When the woman slammed the hood, they were ready to drive away. Their red-haired escort sat behind the wheel and started the engine; all of her movements were efficient without being rushed. She glanced at them in the rearview.

"I'm Sergeant Carol Shepard." She held up her ID. "I'll be taking you to—shit, we've got company!" she said. She gave it gas and squealed toward the exit, but not before Linda saw the tired man throw his coffee aside and draw a gun. It looked huge and obscene in his hands. She had never seen a real gun up close before, and yet there was a sense of déjà vu in the whole experience: Josh's hands pushing her urgently, wanting her out of harm's way; Carol Shepard's stream of swearing as she catapulted onto the street; the noise of gunfire, not like a roar, but like precise buttons of sound.

Linda lifted her head as they careened away. "Are you all right?" Shepard was shouting from the front seat.

It was real, then, Linda thought. All of her fears and suspicions had been justified, and Nob wanted her dead. He wanted her dead. She squinted, trying to focus on the thought, on anything. Josh said nothing, but Linda finally managed, "I'm all right. Is he following us?"

Officer Shepard consulted the rearview again. "He's on foot. By the time he reaches a car, we'll be long gone. Take a deep breath," she advised. "How's your boyfriend?"

Linda was about to say, "He's not my boyfriend," which was both a lie and a superfluous detail, given the circumstances, but she was distracted by the sight of Josh's blood, rapidly staining his shirt and dripping on the seat at her side. "Oh God, oh God," she said. "Josh is shot. He's shot. What do we do?"

Carol Shepard risked a glance into the back seat, then looked back at the road. "He took a bullet in the back, it looks like. Is he conscious?"

Linda lifted his head, her heart plummeting. "No."

"Alive?"

She held his wrist in trembling fingers. "Yes."

"Did the bullet exit? Is there a wound on the front—"

"Yes, yes. And I see here where it went into the front seat."

"That's good," she said. "Try to find something to stop the blood. You have a scarf or something?"

Linda glanced down at her own attire. She yanked off the sweater, found it too bulky, then pulled off the tee. She bundled it, opened Josh's shirt, and pressed it against his wound. He moaned slightly. "Okay," she said.

"You have any CPR experience?" Shepard asked hopefully.

"No," Linda said. "But I'm pressing it against the wound. It's not coming out as fast as I feared," she said bravely.

"That's good. He might have a chance," Shepard said, still calm. "I've got to put some distance between us and our gunman, but I'll radio for an ambulance to meet us in the next town. Okay? We'll get him taken care of."

"I would greatly appreciate that," Linda said, her lips stiff. She would have been amused at her own formality if anything could have been funny in that moment. As it was, she doubted that she would ever smile again. She wiped away a tear, leaving a streak of blood on her face. She was cold, but she dared not let go of Josh's compress to put on her sweater. She sat shivering in her bra, pressing her hand against Josh's heart, and praying.

Paluzzi insisted on waiting in the lobby while Lily and Gray went in. He assumed that the governor wouldn't try anything, not with all these people—God, there were a lot of people!—in various offices and anterooms, milling in the hallway, manning phones, and, in the case of the governor's quarters, sitting behind desks in plush office lobbies. Paluzzi stiffened when the secretary said, "Mrs. Caldwell, the governor will see you now."

Lily gave Tony a thumbs-up, then took Gray's hand and led him toward the large, imposing door at the end of the room. *She's like a little kid going to sit on Santa's lap*, he thought, surprised. *She obviously can't wait to see the guy, to face him.* Paluzzi guessed he couldn't blame her. He felt nervous about the whole thing. It seemed like a setup, but what could Stevens do? His secretary looked like somebody's grandma, and none of these other people seemed aware that this visit had any significance at all.

Still, Tony fingered the gun under his suit jacket. He'd had to show ID to the security men at the entrance and make up some cockamamie story about why he was here. But he was near her, if she needed him, and he was armed. It was best to be prepared for any contingency.

Lily had never met Nob Stevens face to face. When she finally saw him, standing formally behind his desk, she was surprised by two things: how young he looked, despite his age, and how the hatred didn't immediately flow out of her. He came around the desk, a smile pasted on his face, phony as any smile Lily had ever seen, and he extended his hand, politician-like, still grinning. He was saying something, but she didn't hear him, focused as she was on every feature of his face, from the well-trimmed gray brows and the keen blue eyes to the straight nose and the thin mouth—a cruel mouth, Lily decided.

She kept her hands at her sides, and Stevens lowered his. Gray remained behind her. "You know I can't shake your hand, Governor," she said coldly, looking him in the eye. Despite everything, she felt nervous in his presence. Even after a murder, she felt bound by social conventions and rude for breaking them.

"Do I?" asked Stevens, his eyes sparkling with something. Amusement? Anger? Lily wasn't sure. "I'm not sure I know what you mean, but please come in."

He led them to plush chairs, facing each other in a conversational circle. When they sat, Nob Stevens's knees were almost touching hers. It made her feel sick. "Mrs. Caldwell, I'm sure that my note must have interested you. I'm certain that you deserve to be back on the force, and I'm guessing that you'd like to be," Stevens said, genial when he shouldn't have been, in the face of her insult.

Lily shrugged. "I'll get back on the force when my current situation is resolved. I expect that to happen in the next few days. I don't need your intervention, but it's interesting that you offered it. There are plenty of police officers who might like your help. Why give it to me?"

Stevens smiled at her, then at Gray. "I love directness. I can see why your wife appeals to you, Mr. Caldwell. She has spunk." He turned back to Lily, who could feel the sneer forming on her face. "Lily—may I call you Lily?"

She said nothing.

He continued, smoothly, "I may as well tell you that rumors of your suspicions have reached me—suspicions that I was somehow responsible for your shooting and for your partner's death." He switched to a mask of sympathy. Lily almost laughed.

"I must tell you I found it disturbing, although I understand this sort of thing can be a byproduct of trauma—"

"Cut the talk," Lily said, literally unable to stomach more. "We're here because you want to know what we know, and I'll tell you."

She leaned in and stared at those blue eyes, eyes that, to her, seemed suddenly so cold that the temperature in the room was palpably lower. "I know you are Emily Martin's father."

She watched the eyes carefully, those twin blue orbs. They had lost all warmth, but to his credit they didn't change. A muscle twitched in his temple, something so small that it wouldn't normally be noticed. Lily saw it.

Alarmed, Gray started, "Lily—"

She held up her hand, not even looking in his direction. "In addition, I know that you killed Emily Martin and that when my partner and I began to investigate her death, you tried to kill us. In the case of my partner, Danny, you succeeded. You killed him, Stevens, and I'll prove it."

The governor shifted in his chair, then looked at Gray. "Mr. Caldwell, your wife needs help. She needs therapy. I don't wish to presume—"

"Wait, governor. Don't you want to know what else I know?" Lily stared at him. "Or would you like us to leave?"

It was an important moment, and they faced each other for a time, Stevens trying to keep the mask of sympathy but slipping sometimes into annoyance and something more—fear? Lily enjoyed the tension. She felt younger and happier with each moment of Nob Stevens's hesitation. "I suppose you'd better get it all out, Lily. For your own well-being, you probably want to—"

"You're right, this is for my well-being. Because for a whole year no one believed what I told them about you. It was very lonely, Governor. But lately, things have fallen together. At the very time that I found out the truth about your daughter—"

"I never had a daughter."

"And when people started to believe me, your wife disappeared."

144

Stevens's brows went up. *Bang*, Lily thought. *Right between the eyes*. She smiled at him. "And right after the strange disappearance of your wife, Emily Martin's mother was shot in her own home. Shot in the chest, the way I was. Her assailant was aiming to kill. No one asked questions; no one wanted her money or her possessions. It was a shot meant to silence her, just as my shooting was meant to silence me. But here I am, Nob Stevens, and you must be *so* regretting the fact that your aim wasn't better last October the eighth. Yes, I remember the date, because that was the day you tried to end my life."

Lily felt her eyes becoming dry; she had practically stopped blinking in her intense scrutiny of his face, his reactions. He was good. He hid it well, but it was there: in the nervous jangling of the right foot, which he had crossed so casually over his left thigh; in the slight curling of his hands, not into fists, but only because he was exercising great control; and most especially in his expression, which, in its forced geniality, didn't suit the occasion. If he were innocent, he would be scandalized by her accusations and either offended or deeply moved. He was neither. His expression was almost calculating.

Then again, if he were innocent, she wouldn't be in this room.

"Lily," he said, his false smile back in place. "I understand that you're grasping at straws, but you shouldn't try to manipulate my marital problems to suit your purposes. I thought you were an ethical woman."

"Why did you think that?" Lily asked. "I wasn't under the impression that you knew me at all, Governor. It probably makes it easier to kill someone when you don't know them, doesn't it? It must have been much harder for you to kill your daughter."

His eyes narrowed, snakelike, then widened again. The smile never faltered. "I've already told you I—"

"What did Emily know? She'd found out you were her father; that was bad enough. But had she found out everything? Did she confront

145

you with it? Threaten to expose you? Or did she just ask you to love her, to come forward and admit that you were her daddy? You were just a young, up-and-coming politician back then, not the mighty governor. It doesn't seem like too much of a request. She was a nice girl, a smart kid, a good teacher. She was about to become engaged. And she was pregnant."

Stevens stood up in one swift, fluid motion. "Lily, I think you'll agree I've been very patient. I've listened to your bizarre story because, frankly, I felt sorry for you. I'm sorry for what happened to you and sorry that you erroneously placed the blame on me. I've told my security men to leave you alone because I believed you were relatively harmless, that you were just a tragedy of law enforcement.

"But I have to warn you, Lily"—both his tone and his face were full of sudden menace, and Lily saw Gray stiffen in surprise—"if you persist in these allegations, or in your investigation, I'll have no choice but to see that you are silenced."

Gray stood up. He was taller than Stevens. "Don't threaten my wife," he said grimly.

Lily felt almost happy. God, Stevens looked like a guilty man. Not like an angry, innocent one, but like a nervous, oh-so-guilty one. "*Silenced*, Governor? That's such an ominous word!"

"I'll let you see yourself to the door," he said shortly, turning his back on her.

Lily stood, realizing only when her legs almost failed her that she had, in fact, been very nervous. "There's one more thing you should know, Governor. There's a meeting taking place right now, as we speak, that will seal your fate. But don't worry. I'm sure they'll allow spectators at your execution, and you can look at my face if it brings you comfort."

Stevens's back stiffened. "Goodbye, Lily. Good luck to you." His tone was detached, almost apathetic.

146

Gray tried to grab Lily's hand, but she dodged him and ran up to Stevens. She said, right behind his left ear, "Oh, and Nob? That cologne you're wearing? It's the same stuff you were wearing last year when you shot me. I smelled it right before I turned around."

FIFTEEN

"HE MAY AS WELL have confessed to everything," Lily said jubilantly as they climbed into Tony's car. She took shotgun; Gray sat in the back. "He had the guiltiest look I've ever seen—"

She broke off, because Tony was looking to Gray for verification, his eyes flicking to the rearview so that he could bring Gray into his line of vision.

Lily felt the cold wind for the first time. *Here it comes*, she thought. *The double betrayal all over again. Tony can't just believe me, the crazy one. He has to look to Gray, the scientist, the logical presence in the room.* Almost fearfully, Lily observed Gray. His jaw was still clenched, as it had been since they'd left the office.

"He threatened her, Tony," Gray said angrily. "Right in front of me, he threatened my wife, saying he would 'silence' her. What the hell am I supposed to think of that?"

"He said that?" Tony said. He looked back at Lily, who was half-glaring, half-smiling. She couldn't help her euphoria, even in light of Tony's doubt. Tony was, for a rare moment, at a loss for words. He was saved by his cell phone. He took it from his pocket and clicked it on. "Yeah?"

He listened, and Lily watched him. She had missed Tony, missed their daily repartee, missed his bad temper and his swearing and his protective daddy act. Now she recognized a gleam of panic in his eyes. "Shit!" he yelled.

"What?" Lily leaned toward him.

"Keep me updated!" he yelled into his phone, and he clicked off.

"What?" Lily repeated.

Tony slumped in his seat. "Someone got to Mrs. Stevens—"

"*No!*" Lily cried. Then, hesitantly, she asked, "Is she dead?"

Tony sighed and shook his head, including her and Gray in his glance. "No. But her boyfriend got caught in the crossfire, and he might not make it."

———

At a hospital one hour south of Capitol City, Linda sat in a small, secure room with Carol Shepard, her limp right hand in Carol's firm grip. She had put her sweater back on, but she felt permanently cold. Josh's prognosis was uncertain. Aside from her guilt at involving him in her crisis, Linda felt an overwhelming sorrow, a disillusionment with the universe that she could not put into cohesive thought, much less into words. She stared mutely at Sergeant Shepard, who assured her that everything would be all right.

"We've got some people coming out here to see you. My chief, for one—Chief Tony Paluzzi. He wants to ask you some questions about this whole thing you're involved in. He's also bringing some people with him."

Linda lifted her head. "Lily Caldwell?" she asked.

Shepard looked surprised. "I think he mentioned Lily. I thought maybe I heard wrong, but—"

"Why? Because she was fired? Does she have a bad reputation?" Linda was curious now, curious on Josh's behalf, because these were questions he'd been starting to ask the night before.

Shepard shook her head. "It's not for me to say. I don't gossip about my colleagues."

Linda nodded. She stared at a white wall. "Are we safe in here?"

"Yes, ma'am. And there's more security posted outside. He's armed, and so am I."

"Guns," Linda said vaguely. She'd never thought they would be a part of her life, other than something seen on television or something discreetly hidden by the secret service when she and Nob traveled. Now Josh was fighting for his life, gunshot.

She'd met Josh when she'd volunteered to do a charity photo shoot on behalf of a children's hospital. She'd been the spokesperson for their fundraising campaign, and several local celebrities had lent their names, talents, and dollars to the project. Josh, as a noted artist, was one of the people involved. He and Linda had struck up a conversation at a little buffet table on a meeting day and had gone to dinner together later in the week. Linda had found him refreshingly open. When she visited his studio and saw his work, mainly wood and metal sculpture, she was overwhelmed by his talent and vision. She'd been a little in love with him ever since.

She tried to think now why it was that she had wanted Nob Stevens so badly when Josh had been the natural choice all along. It all came down, she thought, to Nob's confidence. It was very attractive, and he'd turned his attention on her like a laser beam, making her feel spoiled. When they spoke of their relationship, Nob was so sure, so certain of her love for him, that she became convinced as well.

Josh had told her more than once how special, how important, she was in his life.

Nob, even when he proposed, didn't say that in so many words. He'd brandished an expensive ring and a megawatt smile and said, "Let's make this official."

She shook her head now, sitting bereft of hope in a room with white walls. The policewoman still held her hand, but Linda didn't feel safe. No one could protect her from her own regrets.

———————

Tony glared at the army behind him. Lily and Gray had insisted on accompanying him, as had Claudia and Harvey. He wanted to question Mrs. Stevens alone, but there was no way he could keep Lily out. She had broken this alone; she'd taken the heat, endured a firing, almost messed up her marriage. Lily was allowed.

The rest of them, he wasn't so sure. He swung around in the empty hallway, near the door that separated them from Linda Stevens. "You can't all be in here," he said. "This is a police interview. She's not going to want reporters in there," he said, looking pointedly at Claudia, "and she doesn't know who the hell any of you are. This will be hard enough for her. She's been hunted by her husband, and her boyfriend might die. Yesterday she was the pretty wife in the mansion, and today she's a fugitive."

Lily stepped forward, her chin thrust out. "I'm going in."

He nodded. "I didn't say *you* couldn't go."

"And Gray should be there. He can explain what Harvey found, if you're not going to let Harvey do it."

Paluzzi sighed. "Fine. Let's go."

Harvey shrugged and handed Gray his envelope, *the* envelope. Gray nodded, exchanging a significant glance with his friend.

He and Lily followed Paluzzi into the room.

What Lily noticed first was how pretty she was and how young she looked. She was almost like a girl, slender and blonde, with small

151

hands and feet. She looked up at them, and Lily saw the misery she herself had felt for so long. It ate from within, and it looked as though it had been working on Linda Stevens for quite some time.

"Mrs. Stevens, I'm Anthony Paluzzi, chief of Homicide for the Capitol City police," Tony said in his formal voice, reaching out his hand and clasping her pale white one. She seemed to be having some trouble focusing. Lily wondered if they'd given her any anxiety medication.

"Hello, Chief Paluzzi." Her voice was soft, very human. She seemed approachable. Lily had expected a celebrity, whatever that meant.

Tony set a tape recorder on the table in the middle of the room. He explained that it was merely for a record of their discussion. He introduced Gray and Lily, then gave the date. Sergeant Shepard had been dismissed. "Mrs. Stevens, we need to ask you some questions about what has happened in the last couple of days: why you left the governor's mansion without a trace, why your husband was so concerned about your absence, why someone tried to kill you this morning."

She nodded, as though waiting for more.

Paluzzi looked puzzled. "Why did you leave your home yesterday, Mrs. Stevens?"

She shrugged, sighed, then looked directly at Lily. "You're Lily?" she asked.

Lily, shocked, answered, "Yes. I spoke with your—with Joshua Randall on the phone."

"Thank you," she said. "Apparently you called just in time."

Lily nodded. "You should also thank John Pierre. He was worried about you."

Linda's elegant brows rose. "John? Well, what do you know. If he's left Nob's side, Nob is in trouble."

"Mrs. Stevens." Paluzzi looked impatient. "Why did you leave your home yesterday?"

She crossed her legs, then wrapped her arms around her body, as though she were cold. "I found something. In our—in my bedroom. It was a letter and some photographs. I—when I read it, I began to harbor a terrible suspicion about my husband. I felt, instinctively, that I had to get away from him, to distance myself from him. I told him a lie. I told him my sister had cancer, and I wanted to go to be with her. It was a good choice. He doesn't like my sister, and he doesn't like to talk about her. He didn't even feel compassion when I mentioned chemotherapy. He was upset that I would leave at a crucial point in his re-election campaign."

There was silence in the room. Lily said, "Why tell him a lie? Why not just say that you needed some space, that you wanted to separate?"

Linda's brows furrowed. "You'd have to know Nob. He'd want reasons, rationalizations, and he's very good at arguing them all away. He's very good at making you second-guess yourself, making you think you were wrong. I didn't have the energy or the desire for one of his debates."

Tony started again, going slowly. "Mrs. Stevens, you mentioned that you were harboring a suspicion. What was the nature of that suspicion, may I ask?"

Linda shook her head. "I can't—even now, I keep thinking I must have made a mistake. I hate to say anything, for fear that I would be—"

"Mrs. Stevens, someone tried to kill you this morning," Paluzzi reminded her.

"Yes," she said, almost apologetically.

"Get angry," Lily said suddenly.

"What?" Linda asked.

"It helps. With the grief and the helplessness. The anger helps you get some power back. You should be very angry at Nob Stevens. God knows I am."

153

Tony glared at her, but Linda seemed to be listening.

Tony started again. "This letter—do you have it with you?"

Linda shook her head. "I put it back. I put them back. Right where I found them. I didn't want him to know."

"Can you tell us what the letter said? Who it was from? Or what the pictures were of?" Tony asked.

She set her hands on her thighs and stared at them. "The pictures were of a woman, a young, naked woman. They were rather old photographs, not very good quality. Some of them—well, she seemed like an unwilling subject in them. Except in the ones where she was sleeping. He took those without her knowledge, I suppose."

"Your husband took them?" Tony asked.

"I assume he did. I—I don't know. The letter seemed to imply—"

"Tell us about the letter," Tony said. Lily leaned forward, unable to contain her eagerness.

Linda was still staring at her lap. "It was from a woman named Cammy."

"Camilla Martin?" Lily said.

"I don't know," Linda said. "She said, in the letter—well, she was upset. Very upset. She wrote—God, it was heart wrenching, but I only realize that now. At the time I was too shocked."

"Why were you shocked?" Tony asked.

She shook her head. "I can't—I find I can't bring myself—"

She looked at them helplessly. Gray stood up and sat in a closer chair. "Mrs. Stevens, my name is Gray. Lily is my wife. She and I are familiar with a woman named Camilla Martin, because Lily was investigating the death of her daughter, a girl named Emily Martin. For reasons of her own, Lily compared the DNA of Emily Martin with that of your husband."

Linda's eyes widened. Lily was reminded of a frightened horse.

"You—how did you—," Linda began.

154

Gray continued smoothly, calmly. "It might help you to talk with us if you know that the results troubled the scientist who examined them. The patterns were similar, but more similar than they would be for a normal father and child. We found, you see, that your husband was the father of Emily Martin."

Linda trembled slightly. "He told me he didn't have children. But this letter—what are you saying? What was wrong with the test?"

Lily was impressed with Linda Stevens's ability to process information even in the wake of several shocks, endured one after another.

Gray opened the file he held. "If you look at the patterns that we have here—Emily's DNA profile, and your husband's—you can see that they are virtually identical. That suggested a parent-child relationship, but it actually suggested . . . more than that."

Linda met his eyes. She had confirmed their suspicions, Lily saw, without even speaking. "What did it suggest?" Linda asked bleakly.

"It suggested that Nob Stevens and the mother of Emily Martin were already related by blood."

The room was silent; the air was pregnant with meaning and menace, with secrets revealed. Linda looked in turn at three of the white walls, restlessly, before she looked back at Gray. "The letter said that. The girl, Cammy—she was his sister. She never wanted—what he did to her. She said, 'Bobby, you must never come near me again.' She mentioned the baby, too, the baby Emily. Nob"—her eyes suddenly filled with tears—"had wanted her to abort it. The baby had been unplanned. I think he had—a long history with his sister. I think she was quite young when it started.

"The girl, Cammy, had agreed never to speak of their—relationship—if he left her and the baby alone. The letter suggested that Nob had been . . . pursuing her still. She was married. She told him to stay away. To keep to their agreement."

Linda stopped, drained and obviously relieved. Her burden was gone, unloaded, and it was now for the three people in the room to do with it what they would.

Tony reached out and took Linda's hand, murmuring softly about how grateful they were for her cooperation and how he would be right back to make arrangements to take her to a safe place. Linda Stevens nodded, then shook her head.

"No—I mean thank you, but I'll want to stay near Josh. I need to be with him."

Tony stood, looking compassionately down at her, even touching her pretty blonde hair. Lily appreciated, suddenly, that sometimes a woman needed a father figure, someone to take the role of caretaker. For once she didn't find this paternal response insulting, perhaps because she was able to see it bestowed on someone else. "We'll make arrangements," Tony said.

In the hall, minutes later, Tony looked at Gray and Lily. "Well, son of a bitch," he said with feeling. "I've got to talk to the DA. Tell your sister to get her ass in gear. This story is coming out whether we want it to or not, and the governor's balls will be in the wringer by tonight."

Claudia and Harvey appeared, and Gray spoke to them briefly. They waved to Lily before linking hands and running after Paluzzi.

Lily laughed in disbelief, looking at Gray, who suddenly took her hand. "God, Lily, it's happening. You thought it never would."

She sobered again. "It doesn't feel as good as it should. I keep thinking of Emily, poor Emily. She must have found out, Gray. How must she have felt? What must she have thought? And then her father killed her."

Gray still held her hand; he pulled her into a warm embrace.

Then they walked silently through the emergency room and out of the hospital, but not before they'd glimpsed several examples of human cruelty: a child with a blackened, swollen eye; a moaning victim of a knifing; and two victims of gang warfare, who never even made it to an operating table but were apparently being wheeled straight to the morgue.

Something inside Lily constricted, causing a pain she couldn't identify, and even the cold October air didn't refresh her. She remembered, suddenly, that when she woke briefly in the ambulance on the night of her shooting, woke to that whole new dimension that was physical pain, someone had said, "You're going to make it! You're going to make it! Stay alive. Stay alive." An ambulance attendant had chanted it as he worked desperately, tearing at her shirt, inserting her IV.

Lily thought of it now, leaning her head against her seat, closing her heavy lids, letting Gray drive her away from the scene and back to Capitol City. *Stay alive. Stay alive*, she thought. It was a mantra worth embracing. *You're going to make it. You're going to make it.*

When she opened her eyes and looked out the window, they were well on their way back home.

SIXTEEN

CLAUDIA LEFT THE MEETING with her chief editor and the owner of the station feeling both euphoric and dissociated from reality. Stories like this never happened, except in movies of the week. Her editor, Chuck, had already spoken with Tony Paluzzi, and despite his shock, he seemed to be floating on air, like Charlie Brown when he thought of the little red-haired girl.

She was about to break the story on national television, and it was her exclusive. An exclusive. Claudia had never had one, certainly not one this big. Featuring prominently in her coverage would be a young former police officer named Lily Caldwell; Chuck had told Claudia that it wasn't a conflict of interest as long as she revealed her relationship at the beginning of the report. *In the interest of full disclosure, I must report that Lily Caldwell is my sister-in-law.*

She went over her notes as she sat in the makeup chair. She felt strangely calm, yet frightened in a deep, soul-scorching way. This story affected everyone. Not just her or her station or Lily and Gray, or even the governor himself. It affected, it seemed to her, everyone in the country, if not the world. When Watergate broke, it made Americans forever suspicious of their presidents. What would this do to their perception of politicians, of whom they were already mistrustful? To their ability to trust at all?

The makeup woman moved away, and Claudia floated to her desk. The camera was poised, ready to record her, to register this moment for posterity. Ben's eyes were bulging at her in disbelief; he had been reading her notes. She gave him a wan smile and faced the camera. She watched the cameraman's fingers as they counted down. Three, two, one . . .

"Good evening, everyone. I'm Claudia Caldwell. Our top story this evening is a Channel Seven exclusive. It involves alleged crimes committed by Governor Robert Stevens against several people, some of which go all the way back to the governor's teen years. Police are currently investigating Governor Stevens for allegations of rape and murder.

"We must begin, first of all, by going back to a homicide committed last year, a crime that involved two Capitol City police officers . . ."

———————

Even in reduced circumstances, in hiding and portrayed to the world as some sort of monster, Nob Stevens could smile. To begin with, because he had outsmarted the world for so long and was outsmarting them again; long ago he'd made certain that he'd have somewhere safe to go if the worst happened. He'd walked right out of his office soon after Lily's visit. He'd packed some necessities into his briefcase, called for his car, and even stopped to chat with people on his way out, knowing he had a bit of time. In a final, grand gesture, he'd grabbed Tammy, the girl who'd had a crush on him for two years, and pulled her into a hallway for a long, lascivious kiss. The look on her face still made him smile: shock, disbelief, and something like loathing. She'd seemed much more attractive to him after that. Too bad he didn't have time to pursue it . . .

Now he sat in comfort, watching the television and feeling something between horror and pride as images of himself flashed on the screen, one after the other: images of his youth, his early career in law, his swearing-in ceremony, even his goddamn wedding picture. He shook his head and took a sip of his Scotch.

When Cammy's picture appeared on the screen, he froze. They'd found one from her youth, a picture he didn't think he'd ever seen before. She might have been sixteen when it was taken. God, she'd been beautiful, with her long, wavy hair and her curving body. She'd belonged to him then, to him exclusively. Their father had left long before, and their mother had died around the time Nob turned eighteen. She'd never suspected his relationship with Cammy, or if she had, she had avoided any confrontation. She'd had cancer to contend with. So Nob had been left alone with his glorious obsession, his lovely Cammy. Only George Martin had changed that—and the pregnancy that never should have happened.

As if in response to Nob's bitter thoughts, a picture of Emily flashed before him. Claudia Caldwell, the reporter, began the sob story: "A life destined to be cut short. Police are planning to reopen the investigation of Emily Martin's death now that it has been alleged that she was Governor Stevens's daughter—a daughter, it is suggested, that he conceived with his own sister."

Lord, how he hated that smug look on her face. He was contemplating some sort of revenge against Claudia Caldwell when he heard her say, "In an interview taped earlier, I was able to discuss the allegations with the woman who has pursued the case for a year—former Capitol City police officer Lily Caldwell."

There she was, with her little white triangle of a face and that dark hair that always looked slightly uncombed. He despised her. She looked sober and thoughtful, not at all malicious, as she'd looked in his office while she stabbed at him with her little knives of information. *If only she'd died,* he thought. *If only she'd died that night as she was meant to do.*

He took another sip of Scotch and closed his eyes, allowing the alcohol to warm and calm him. He wished he could call Cammy to ask her what she thought about it all. It was Lily's fault that he'd had to hurt Cammy at all; she'd been content to live her silent life, ever loyal to him and refusing to implicate him in anything society would consider shocking. Society damn well didn't understand. Poor Cammy. He wondered if she would live. If she did, he could seek her out in the future, live with her perhaps, after he got rid of that fucking Martin, who had stolen her from him once before.

With a sigh, he began to relax. Nob had never been one to dwell on conflict. He was all about resolution. It was the only way to be successful, and he firmly believed that he would be successful again. This would all die down, the way it always did for celebrities. If Lily Caldwell died, the opposition would most likely die with her, he told himself. Even if it didn't, he felt it was only right that she should die. She had been a thorn in his side since—

"Governor Stevens, I firmly believe, is a sick, cruel man who has hidden his dirty secrets behind his slick smile and his clever repartee," Lily Caldwell was saying. The camera had closed in so that her face filled the screen. "And the moment we began to uncover those secrets, people started dying again," she said, her red mouth curving into a judgmental frown.

Nob threw his glass at the television. It didn't shatter, but rather bounced onto the rug and spilled the remaining fluid into the carpet fibers. "Bitch. You nosy little bitch," he said. He hadn't planned to leave his safe house for a time. He still had to dye his hair and alter his appearance as best he could. He needed to lie low, he supposed, until he could come up with a game plan. He had time, and he had a place to stay. He'd even had the foresight to stock it well with food and any-thing else he might need. There was no reason he had to leave this dwelling. Not for weeks, perhaps.

Lily Caldwell, though—she was reason enough. He would leave at night. He would make a plan, and he would be careful. He'd always been careful. He'd carved a career from the ability to make the right decisions, to be canny and smart. Killing Mrs. Caldwell, Nob thought, with sudden, cold clarity, was the right decision.

Linda watched the TV in Joshua Randall's private hospital room; she stared until she couldn't bear it, and then she held up the remote and flicked away the sound and the picture, but the images remained. The room seemed unbearably silent. She felt jumpy, itchy under her skin. Josh hadn't regained consciousness but lay instead like a dead man, surrounded by machines. Things that beeped and hissed were her only companions. Outside the door, she knew, a man with a uniform and a gun stood sentry. It was unlikely that Nob would come here or anywhere public, but that man who had shot Josh was a hireling, and Nob could have an endless number of them.

She felt a certain horror—not of what Nob would do, but of what he was. She had never really known him—she understood that now—but she'd lived with him, and she'd been more intimate with him than any other person. She'd been his only wife. At first she had thought that was romantic: after fifty-five years he'd finally found a woman to whom he wanted to commit the rest of his life. Romantic. Linda shiv-ered, though the room was unusually warm.

She rubbed her arms, but her skin felt raw, almost painful, as though it wasn't enough to cover her body. The thought of skin, human skin, suddenly made her want to cry. An image of Lily Caldwell entered her mind. She had liked Lily Caldwell. She remembered Lily looking at her and saying, "Get angry." Lily, she mused, wouldn't sit around and let life get to her. Lily had been fighting all along, Linda realized. From what she'd heard on the news, Lily had gone up against impossible odds to try to find out Nob's secrets. She had suffered personal losses and a lack of support from her friends, even from her husband.

Ultimately, it seemed, Lily Caldwell had believed in herself and in her mission.

Linda reached out to touch Josh's arm. To have a mission in life: was that what brought one happiness? Was Lily Caldwell happy? Or was she just angry? Would her anger fade now that Nob had been exposed?

Linda remembered wryly that when she'd been a young model, many things had made her angry. Shoots that took too long. Rude photographers. Models with seemingly less talent and professionalism who were paid more than she was. Men who looked for sex instead of human companionship. At times, when she was young, she got angry just for the pleasure of it, just to revel in the power of her own indignation. Somehow, early on, that was how she proved that she was an individual, someone who knew her own mind. Anger was a luxury she indulged in, like manicures or highlights or facials.

She realized, as she held Josh's hand, that she hadn't really been angry in years. She'd been resigned, depressed, but never angry.

Josh's arm was bright yellow under the tape of his IV. Some sort of antiseptic, she knew, but it made him seem more ill, as though he'd become permanently jaundiced. She felt bitterness bubbling up in her as she stared at that yellow skin. It was power; it was like an engine starting—an engine that had been cold too long.

Linda had grown up on a farm in Iowa. Not many people knew it about her, and she barely believed it about herself, so long ago had it been. She had a sudden image now of her father, after his morning coffee and cigarette, dressed in insulated overalls and a deerskin cap, ready to take the car for a weekly trip into town. Linda always went along; as the youngest, she was the most pampered and the one who most craved the "bigness" of places other than the farm. "Let's hope it starts, Lindy," he'd say to her with a wink.

Sometimes it didn't start, and her father would swear, slam out of the car, and lift the hood. Most times, though, like a miracle, that motor would purr, and Linda would wonder vaguely what made it happen, how turning that key made some mysterious life occur in the engine. Her dad would hum "Old Gray Bonnet" and navigate the ruts and bumps of their driveway with a jovial demeanor.

She was suddenly overwhelmed with a strong yearning to see both her father, who lived still on that farm and who she hadn't seen in two years, and the land itself, that big, endless stretch of lonesomeness that now seemed like paradise, looking back.

It was that old car engine she thought of when she felt the rumbling inside herself, the rumbling and the power that had for so long failed her. Anger *was* a luxury—it was—and coming after so long an absence, it was like birth.

She stood next to Joshua, and when his eyes opened she was looking at him with determination, her hands clenched on his thin hospital blanket.

SEVENTEEN

When Lily and Gray arrived home, a mob of reporters was camped outside their house.

"We should have anticipated this," Gray said. "Do you want to talk to them?"

Lily yawned. "No. You go first and beat them away. You're a man."

"Thanks for noticing," he said, opening his door. She got out, too, and darted behind him, staying close to his back as he repeated, "No comment," over and over, even shoving one persistent cameraman out of the way so that they could reach their door unmolested.

Once they were inside, Lily looked at him in disbelief. "I didn't want all this," she said. "I just wanted him to pay."

Gray took her hand and led her to the kitchen, where he began to root around. "When's the last time you ate, Lily?"

She shrugged, sitting wearily at the table. "I can't really remember. Between the meeting with Stevens this morning and the meeting with Linda this afternoon—I'm not sure we ate at all, did we?"

Gray sighed. "I suppose not. I think Harvey handed me part of a sandwich at the hospital. Let's see what we have in here. I did manage to buy some food before all the shit hit the fan. I assume Tony no longer thinks you beat up his car," he said, smirking into a cabinet.

"He never did. They actually came for me before Tony knew about it. About the prints, I mean. Anyway. He was mostly angry that my investigation was making things happen. Maybe he was angry at himself."

Gray turned to her suddenly, holding a can of tomatoes. "I know that feeling, Lily. With all this happening"—he gestured to the reporters who still stood on their lawn—"the whole world knows that you were right. Like I should have known a long time ago."

Lily examined the napkin holder, the same one that had been debugged. "There was no evidence then."

"Except your word." Suddenly he was kneeling in front of her. "I know you haven't fully forgiven me, and I can understand that. I see the immensity of it all, and I think of what a burden you were bearing—God, Lily. I don't know what to say."

She looked up. "Say you love me."

"I love you. I've always loved you, and I always will."

"Say you're sorry."

"I'm sorry." He lifted her hands and kissed them. "I really am."

"Say everything will be all right." Her eyes glistened with tears.

"Everything will be great. And you don't have to be a toughie anymore, Lily. No one ever expected you to be emotionless. I think it's good for you—crying now and then."

"Gray." She wiped at her eyes. "Make some food before we starve."

He jumped up and went back to his work at the counter. Within minutes he'd chopped some chicken and vegetables into a pan; Lily closed her eyes and savored the spicy smell of peppers frying. "Mmm. Now I know I'm hungry," she said. She opened her eyes and ventured to the window. "They're almost all gone. It's getting dark. Claudia will be on the five o'clock news soon."

"Do you want to watch it?" he asked, stirring, not meeting her eyes.

"No." She came back to him. "I want to eat and relax and avoid all thoughts of this now."

Gray nodded. "Why don't you pour some wine?"

"Okay. From our vast cellars?"

"I bought a couple cheap ones at the store. I suppose white would go better with this."

Lily went to their small wine holder and examined Gray's purchases. He had chosen well and stayed within a budget. He was definitely more of a homemaker than she had ever been. She felt suddenly as though she'd underestimated him, as though she'd taken him for granted even before she'd been shot. She found a corkscrew and opened the wine, then poured it into two glasses. She brought one to Gray. He clinked it against hers. "I think we should throw you a little party, Lily."

"I don't think so." She smiled, shaking her head.

"Just a few people. Claudia and Harvey. Tony and some people from the force. Maybe . . . your mom."

Lily's eyebrows went up. "That's a motley group."

"They all wish you well."

"I don't know . . ."

"In a few days you'll feel rested. You'll feel ready to hear the acknowledgments and the apologies. You may not want to talk to reporters, Lily, but you've got to let some people eat crow. I'll make a nice dinner, and we'll ask them—"

"Maybe. We'll see. Let's just sit down with our wine." She took his free hand and led him to the couch. They sat down and looked at each other for a minute. Lily felt that his emotions were in almost as much turmoil as her own. His gray eyes looked darker in the dim room.

"Dinner will be ready in ten minutes," he said.

"I wonder if I'll still be awake."

"Kind of early for bed."

Lily touched his hair. "Not if you go with me." She knew he was back to stay, no matter how badly she had treated him. She knew he was a loyal man who had made one mistake. She knew that she loved him. She thought of him as he faced Nob Stevens, as he glared into his face and said, "Don't threaten my wife."

Gray set down his wine, then took her glass and put it carefully beside his. He turned back to her. "You want me?"

"Yes. I want you to come back to me. I want you to stay. I'm sorry I've been—"

He held up his hand. "I deserved it. Lily, there's nothing I want more than to be your husband again. You know that." He leaned closer, easing his arms around her. "You're too thin, babe. I need to fatten you up," he said, pressing his hands against her tiny waist.

She laughed, her face just under his. "I haven't eaten your cooking in a long time."

"Now things will be different." He lowered his head until his lips touched her hair. He moved gently, so gently she could barely feel him there, but she grew warm all over at that butterfly touch.

"Gray, I'm worried," she said, closing her eyes as his mouth moved to her right ear.

"About what?" he asked.

"Where is he? They haven't caught him. Where could he possibly hide? He's known all over the—"

He put a finger over her lips. "You said you didn't want to think about that."

"I know." She took a deep breath, and by the time she exhaled, his mouth was on hers. With a little moan and a luxurious melting feeling, she leaned into him and let him lead her. He kissed her, gently but thoroughly, until he suddenly pushed her away and jumped up.

"Shit. Sorry, babe, but dinner is gonna burn," he yelled over his shoulder as he ran toward the kitchen.

Lily giggled and settled into her spot on the couch. Moments later, Gray brought her a steaming bowl on a dinner tray. She couldn't remember ever having been this hungry or food ever tasting so good. They didn't speak until Lily was finished eating.

"More?" Gray asked, watching her.

She reached for her wine. "No. That was delicious, husband. I'm glad the cook is back on the ranch."

He gave her a searching look. "I'm going to run you a bath. You need to relax. Now that you've got some nutrients in your system, it's time to pamper you. Okay?"

"Okay," she said. She was suddenly very willing to be pampered.

Gray kissed her and said, "I'll be right back."

She leaned back on the sofa and closed her eyes again; she must have fallen asleep, because the next thing she knew, Gray was carrying her upstairs. "What?" she said to him.

"I was going to put you in bed, but since you're awake, I guess I'll stick you in the tub. It's a perfect temperature, and it smells nice."

She let her head fall against his chest. "*You* smell nice."

Gray set her feet down on the bathroom tile. "Do you want me to help you get undressed?"

"That's such a line," she joked. "And yes."

He did, more rapidly than either of them had intended. By the time he was finished, the mirror was steamier than the bath water had made it. "Get in with me," she gasped, breaking away from his kisses as his hands roamed the landscape of her body.

169

"Not relaxing that way," he protested feebly.

"Much more relaxing in the long run," she said, nibbling his ear.

He didn't protest further.

————————

When Claudia's report ended and she started toward her office, she saw Harvey waiting for her. She felt a sudden warm gladness before her brain told her not to get excited. "Hello," she said warily.

Harvey bounded forward and caught her up in a rib-crushing embrace. "You were great!" he yelled, swinging her fully around before setting her down.

Claudia laughed, her eyes darting up and down the hall at various colleagues who were, to her relief, smiling at the sight. "Let's go into my office," she said, embarrassed.

They did, hand in hand because Harvey wouldn't let go of hers. "I mean it, Claudia, you were cool as a cucumber, and when you put it all together like that, well, it looked mighty damning." He sat in a chair across from her desk and pulled her onto his knee.

"Harvey!" she said, her face hot. "I'm trying to be professional here."

He raised his eyebrows, still smiling. "Why? You're not interviewing me."

"No." She tried to stand up but failed to extricate herself. "But I'm at work."

He nodded, his face suddenly falling. "God, you're going to get a million calls after this, aren't you? From CNN or *The View* or some New York powerhouse media thing. Everyone will want you, because you broke this story."

She shook her head. "I didn't break anything. It was handed to me. I was lucky enough to know Lily, that's all. Lily's the one who—"

Harvey looked crestfallen. "You'll be so busy you won't give me the time of day."

For the first time since she'd met him, she felt the need to encourage him. "Harvey, you know that's not true. If you think that of me, then you shouldn't want to be with me, anyway."

He ran a finger down her arm. "It's not that simple, Miss Claudia."

The shiver that went through her made her feel bold. "So when is dinner?"

"Hmm?"

"The dinner that you said you wanted with me. Tablecloths, silverware, music. Wasn't that what you promised?"

"It was." He smiled at her, and she noticed slight dimples that she hadn't seen before. "How about tonight? Now?"

She felt chagrin. It sounded so good all of a sudden. "I have to do this again for the ten o'clock news. Do you believe in late dinners?"

He feigned the pose of someone in deep thought, his chin in his hand. "I could consider it. If my companion were pretty."

"She is," Claudia said.

He laughed. "Fine. I'll eat a sandwich so I don't starve to death waiting. In the meantime, can I hang out here and watch you work?"

She tried again to leave his lap, but he pulled her into a sudden kiss. His lips were warm and surprisingly sweet, and she found that she didn't want to break away, as was usually her instinct, ever since Ben. She leaned in, touching his hair, and he made a sound that had her wishing this weren't the day she had broken the biggest story in the world, but just a regular, quiet evening that would allow her to go home, relax, and make love if she so chose. "Harvey," she said. She even liked his name better now.

"Can I stay?" he asked again, his lips against hers.

She leaned away, with such reluctance that he smiled. She stood and walked toward the work piled on her desk. "If you help me. I need updates on Camilla Martin's and Joshua Randall's conditions. We need to check with Paluzzi about what's being done to find the governor. And we need more background info on the man. We need childhood friends and acquaintances who knew him and his sister—"

"Isn't that what all those peons are on the phone about?" Harvey gestured to the newsroom outside her office.

She grinned. "Most of them. But you can join the fray. If you want to hang around, you must earn your keep."

"Only if I get to stare at you while I do it." He stood, too, looking suddenly tall and masculine. She was trying not to picture him naked, but it was only sort of working.

"You're very flattering. Some women find that insincere," she warned, sorting through the paper on her desk, trying to hide her sudden burst of desire.

"But you don't, because you know you're attractive and you know that I have a thing for you," he said calmly, perching on the edge of her desk and flipping idly through her *Far Side* calendar. "And I'll tell you right now, so that you can think about it in your reporter's brain. Tonight, after our late dinner, I'm going to ask you to go to bed with me. I'm giving you plenty of time to dream up denials and excuses, but I am also allowing you some freedom to contemplate the possibilities. I don't want to sound pompous, but I'm confident I could show you a good time."

"I believe that," she said softly, stunned by his comment but not at all displeased.

"Why, Claudia Caldwell, you have a very naughty look on your face!" he said, leaning toward her.

"No more kissing," she said briskly, picking up her phone. "I have a job to do."

She handed him a sheaf of papers, trying to wear a stern expression. "File these," she said, pointing to a cabinet.

Harvey laughed loudly, but he did the filing, quickly and efficiently. That was when she realized that she would say yes. There was no need for him to know that, though. She frowned down at her blotter and dialed the Capitol City police.

EIGHTEEN

NOB STEVENS WAS STILL missing two weeks later. He was the biggest news story in recent memory. If Capitol City had ever known a more significant scandal, Lily wasn't aware of it. She had stopped dreaming about him, and so far she hadn't dreamed again about Danny, either. Gray thought she might still want to talk to her old therapist, but Lily said she would wait and see. She was feeling stronger, feeling her old sense of power, and it made her healthier inside and out. Two weeks of Gray's cooking had put some meat back on her bones, and she had called her mother and enjoyed a constructive conversation with her.

Things were good, very good, and she had agreed to Gray's party idea. Why not allow some people back into her life? They would have to acknowledge now that she wasn't crazy, and she wouldn't have to fear what secret suspicions were harbored about her sanity every time she met someone's eyes.

On a Friday at noon Lily met with Tony Paluzzi to discuss her reinstatement ceremony. Tony had admitted that the police force had been in error in the firing of Lily; he had done so in a televised press conference, during which he had asked for Lily's pardon on behalf of the entire Capitol City police force. Many old comrades had called Lily to apologize personally, including Sharon Gonzalez, her old ice cream pal. After a while, Lily let the machine take the apologies. There was only so much of that she could listen to, and it didn't feel as good as she thought it might.

Now Tony glared at her in his usual way. "Are you listening? Or are you daydreaming? Being the hero going to your head?"

"No, Ton. I just have a lot on my mind. I'm going to the doctor after this, and then I've got errands to run. And Gray and I have company coming tonight, including you, if you and Ellen are . . . ?"

"Yeah, yeah, we'll be there. I told your husband yesterday. Now, do you have any questions about the ceremony?"

"No." Lily stared absently at her lap.

"Lil. You *are* glad to be coming back, aren't you? Because I'm really glad to have you, okay? I missed you like hell."

She looked up, surprised, gratified, then leaped out of her chair to plant a kiss on his whiskery cheek. Tony laughed, embarrassed. Then he frowned. "Why are you going to the doctor?"

"What?"

"Are you sick or something? Is it your bullet wound, or—"

"No, no, Ton. It's just a checkup. I basically haven't gone since I left the hospital, so I figured I'd get, you know—"

"Yeah, okay. I'll see you tonight, kid."

"Right. Bring an appetite." She sent him her new smile, the one that didn't feel tortured, and then left the office. Many ex-colleagues waved at her on her way out; some even stood to congratulate her. On her first visit to Tony, the entire office had applauded. Lily still blushed when receiving these accolades, but she tried to feel deserving as well.

It was cold outside, mid-November, and Lily zipped her jacket and consulted her watch. One o'clock. So much to do . . .

175

She had given up her private-investigation job. Capitol City had offered her back pay for her time off the force. She and Gray were debating what to do with the money. They thought they might like to take a vacation together before Lily started back to work.

It would have to be soon, Lily thought, for a lot of reasons.

By two o'clock she had left her doctor's office and was feeling even more absent-minded than she had felt before. She was pregnant—her gynecologist had confirmed it—and she couldn't decide how it made her feel. She and Gray hadn't discussed it, not really, but they'd been making love since the middle of October, when he'd come back and told her about Archie Halsted.

She sat in her car and looked at her shopping list, but she saw nothing. Who was it who said that the only thing you could count on in life was change? That was certainly true, and the changes were so fast and furious that she couldn't process them all.

Pregnant. She wondered how it would affect her career on the force. Would Gray protest? Would Tony be angry? Would she be a good mother?

She shook her head. It would all work out. She would talk to Gray, and he would be calm and rational, the way he always was. And he would be happy. She knew he would. She was smiling to herself when the phone rang.

"Lily? It's Claudia. Is it okay to call you on your cell?"

"Sure. I'm in my car."

"Listen, Lily, I have some bad news."

Lily stiffened. "What?"

"We just heard on the wire: Camilla Martin died today. She never regained consciousness."

"She died? She's dead?" Lily crumpled the list in her hand.

"Yes. Her husband is going to hold a press conference tonight. He said he wants to tell his wife's story now that it can no longer hurt her. He says he wants the world to know what she suffered."

"God," Lily said. The bleakness was back, the helpless feeling. He had won again, claimed another victim, a victim from whom he'd already taken too much. It was as though he'd killed her twice, Lily mused.

"Lily? Are you okay?" Claudia sounded worried.

"Oh. I'm just—thanks for telling me. It's better that I heard it from you." She stared at the crumpled paper in her hand.

"The good news is that Joshua Randall is leaving the hospital today. Mrs. Stevens still hasn't made a comment to the press, but she'll be releasing one through her personal assistant today. Guess who that is?"

Lily shook her head, staring out the window of her car. It had started to rain. "Who?"

"John Pierre."

Lily sniffed. "He bounces right back. Well, good for him." She felt suddenly resentful of Claudia, John Pierre, and Linda Stevens. This had been her happy moment, and it was ruined. Nob Stevens had intruded again. She roused herself enough to say, "Will I see you tonight?"

"Oh, Lily, I wouldn't miss it for the world!" Claudia said.

"And will Harvey be there?"

Her tone changed suddenly. "I wouldn't know—I mean, I'm not familiar with his schedule—"

Lily laughed. As quickly as it had been taken, some of her good humor was restored. "Guess what, Claudia? Gray and I have eyes, and we have functioning brains. And we know how new lovers look, because we sort of are, too. I think you have terrific taste." With a rare attempt at female bonding, she added, "Is he good in bed?"

She could almost hear Claudia blushing. "Lily! I mean, what are you—I don't even know what you and Gray think, but—oh, I've got to go, my producer is waving at me. I'll see you tonight, and I'll try to find out about Harvey."

Lily was laughing again when Claudia hung up.

———————

She stopped briefly at home to take a nap. She would run the errands later, she thought, as she lay in blissful relaxation on her bed. When she heard the door open, she sat bolt upright and began to fumble with her right sock. Then she heard Gray's voice.

"Lily?"

"Up here," she called, her voice only quavering slightly, the relief making her weak enough to fall back on her pillow.

He entered the bedroom, looking surprised. "Do you feel okay, hon? You've been napping a lot. Do you think this might be sort of a delayed reaction?" He sat on the edge of the bed and patted her leg.

"To what?"

"To stress. Everything," he said.

"No." She smoothed her blanket, her expression smug. "There's a much simpler reason for this."

Gray didn't bite. "Hey, I got the rest of the day off. So now I can start early on my pasta—what do you mean?"

"Hmm?" Lily closed her eyes.

"What do you mean, there's a simpler explanation?"

"Oh, for my tiredness, I meant."

"What is it?"

"Tiredness?" She could barely suppress a giggle. She opened her eyes again to enjoy his consternation.

"No, Lily." He was getting that stern look of his. It was very sexy. He was still wearing his glasses, the ones he wore at work, and he looked like an impatient teacher. "I mean, what's the *explanation* for your tiredness."

"Oh, that. Well, I guess it's because I'm pregnant." She grinned at him, hugging a pillow to herself.

Gray stared for a full thirty seconds. For a man so brilliant, he took forever to process some things. "You're pregnant," he said finally.

"With our baby. About one month pregnant. I think we may have conceived that very first time, Gray. Remember, when we made love on the couch down there? When you told me how much you missed me, and—"

"I remember," he said hoarsely, pulling her to him. "God, Lily. A baby!" He kissed her hard, then pulled her back away from him, looked at her, then kissed her again. "How long have you known?"

"Just today. I suspected for a week or so, and then I went to Dr. Basile, and she confirmed it. I saw it, even, on an ultrasound. It doesn't look like much, but you can see it, Gray. We made something together." She smiled at him, suddenly much happier than when she'd first found out.

"A baby." Gray shook his head, grinning like a fool. Then he tightened his grip on her. "Do you feel okay?"

"Just tired. I started suspecting when I kept wanting to come up here and sleep. You know I'm not that type."

"I know," he said, kissing her again.

"Are you happy?" she asked when he stopped.

"I'm ecstatic! Are you?"

"Yes. I really am. I'm scared witless, but I'm—I'm glad, Gray."

He sat up straighter. "We should cancel tonight. If you're feeling tired—"

She laughed, so hard that he laughed a little, too. "Gray, I'm not going to lie here for the whole pregnancy! I'm just taking a little nap. I want tonight. I want to tell everyone. I want to tell the whole world."

He nuzzled her neck. "Can I still make love to you? Is it—okay?"

"Of course."

"Lily." He pushed her back onto her pillow. "Go to sleep now, before I get ideas. I'll go start on my dinner."

"I'll get some supplies after my nap."

"Maybe you shouldn't go out," he said, but then he saw her expression and said, "Okay. Thanks. I appreciate you running some errands." He walked toward the door, then turned and looked at her. "Lily?"

"Hmm?"

"I'm proud of you."

She sat up. "What?"

"You beat the odds. You beat death, Lily. And now you're making a life."

She nodded. "We made it, you and me. I'm just . . . giving it a home."

———————

It was dark when Lily left the grocery store. She called Gray on her cell phone, as he had instructed, making a careful circuit around her car before getting inside. "I'm leaving now, Chef Grayson," she joked.

"Good. Did you get the different cheeses? And the wine—"

"I got everything on the list," she assured him. "And I just made sure no one is under my car, and now I'm coming home."

"Love you," he said.

"Love you." She switched off the phone and loaded her groceries, then started the engine and pulled out of the lot. She was in Gray's Jeep, and it made her feel safer than her own little compact car. She wasn't too concerned about driving, because she knew that Nob Stevens wouldn't want to show himself in a heavily populated area, even at night. The only strip that bothered Lily was the forest preserve road that she had to drive through for about five minutes on her way home, the same road on which Danny had met his death. It had no streetlights, wasn't well traveled, and felt eerie even when a murderer wasn't at large.

When she got there she navigated the road carefully. It was still wet from the morning's rain. She was forced to drive more slowly than she normally would have; she turned on her radio for comfort, and John Fogerty sang lustily into the car, cheering her. She sang along with the refrain, sort of faked her way through it, and was just starting to feel calm when her car twisted out of her control. She did some quick maneuvering on the steering wheel and kept it from going into the oncoming lane. At first she thought she'd skidded on water, hydroplaned because she was going too fast. "But I wasn't going that fast," she murmured, even as she heard the strange sound coming from the car's rear panel. "Shit!" she yelled. She had a flat tire.

She had no choice but to pull over on the shoulder and walk around to the back of her car. The tire had burst; there was no way she could drive home on it, she realized, without bending Gray's rims out of shape. She swore softly. She hadn't changed a tire in ages. She knew how to do it, but she didn't relish doing it here.

She squatted down to look at the damage; the instant she realized the truth, she heard the footsteps behind her.

"You shot it," she said.

NINETEEN

"GIVE THE LADY A cigar," said Nob Stevens. She hadn't turned around, but she knew that voice from meeting with him—and from her nightmares. Wasn't this one of them? The rain-wet street, the darkness, the sound of his sardonic laughter behind her? In the dreams she was always facing away, never confronting him.

She summoned her courage and spun around, expecting to see the gun that would shoot her again, that would take her life this time, but he merely stood there, his hands at his sides. He held a gun, though; she saw it reflecting her tail lights. She barely recognized him in the darkness. His gray hair was black, and he wore casual clothing, jeans and a sweatshirt. "Why?" she asked.

"Big question," he said. "Why what? Why am I going to kill you?"

Lily's throat was suddenly too dry for speech. She nodded. She saw, with something like relief, that he seemed willing to talk for a while. She knew that about Nob Stevens. He needed to hear his own voice, and he'd been alone for two weeks.

He motioned her toward the woods. She began to walk, and he followed. Her phone was in the car; her purse was in the car. How clever he had been again. "Well, Lily Caldwell, I've hated you for a long time. You have to admit that you had many opportunities to let it go. I even offered you one last one, just a few weeks ago, now didn't I?"

She nodded again.

"I can't hear you," his voice said behind her.

"Yes," she said, throwing it over her shoulder.

"Stop here," he said. They were in a cluster of trees, well away from the road. She stood in some wet, rotting leaves, and the scent made her feel nauseous. She was watching the gun, which still wasn't pointing at her.

The queasiness reminded her of something else, and she found her voice. "I'm pregnant," she said. It hurt to talk, like a knife in her dry throat, but she rasped on. "Just like Emily was, but not so far along. Do you enjoy killing babies? I suppose if you killed your own, you don't mind killing other people's."

He looked almost amused. "Lily, you're a strange woman. Not at all feminine, although I can see your beauty more tonight than I could before. You've filled out a bit. It's flattering; that's evident even in the dark. No, don't scream. If you scream, you'll die much sooner."

His tone horrified her more than the words. It was matter-of-fact, no more urgent than if he were telling her what time it was.

"I won't scream," she said, lifting her chin. "I wouldn't give you the satisfaction."

He chuckled, leaning against the tree, his gun finally pointed toward her. "This is all your fault, you know. The shootings."

"Emily—that was my job. It was just my job. And my partner's. He chose the case at random." She heard a tremor creeping into her voice and took a deep breath.

183

"You may as well have shot them yourself," he said, ignoring her. "I certainly wouldn't have taken action otherwise. You were the catalyst. You made it all happen."

The strangest part of the whole scene, she thought, was not the unreality of the dark woods or the moral irresponsibility of his words, but rather the fact that she was starting to believe him. She struggled against the seductive lure of guilt, clenching her fists.

"You've been a criminal for so long you don't even understand what's wrong anymore. When was the first time you raped your sister? Was she twelve? Fourteen?"

"It wasn't rape." For the first time his voice seemed agitated. It sounded gritty, like a mouthful of sand.

Lily persisted, going on instinct. "What do you call it, then? She didn't want it. Did you get off on that? Her protests? Her tears? Her helplessness? I'll bet you told her she couldn't tell anyone, because they would be ashamed of her. I've read whole books about people like you. You know why? Because at the academy we had to study *abnormal* psychology. That's you."

He laughed mirthlessly. "You don't understand anything. I loved her. She's the only one I—"

"She was your sister!"

"Who are you to judge? You slept with your mother's boyfriend. A father figure. We all have our compulsions." His eyes glinted at her in the dark.

"You—," she started. She gasped for breath. "He raped me. It was rape. God, don't you understand what that is?"

He shrugged, then smiled. His teeth looked sickly white in the darkness. "Why don't we do a little role playing? I'll do something to you, and you tell me if it's rape." He moved toward her, his gun steady.

She began to tremble. It was her dream, the dream where he laughed and laughed, and she was helpless to stop him, to prevent his violation. "No," she said. "I don't feel well."

He laughed. "That's a shame, Lily. I'm guessing you'll be feeling worse in a little while. Unless you learn to appreciate my skill." His hand was on her shoulder, pushing her down.

———————

"Where's the lady of the hour?" asked Harvey, perusing the buffet table. "Shouldn't she be descending the stairs in a shimmering gown?"

Gray sniffed. "You don't know Lily very well, do you?"

Harvey laughed. "I think I'm starting to. Is she upstairs? I'll go hassle her."

Gray frowned. "She was running errands." He looked at his watch. "She called half an hour ago to say she was leaving Jewel. The one on Grace Street."

"Hmm. She a careful driver?" asked Harvey.

"I'm getting worried," Gray said. He and his friend exchanged a glance.

"I'll go after her," Harvey said. "What's the route? Straight through the forest preserve?"

Gray leaned against the table, suddenly overwhelmed by a thought. "There's no way he could know, is there? I mean, it would be too risky to follow her around. He couldn't—"

Harvey held up a hand. "Calm down. She could have met a friend, chatted for a while. She could have a flat."

"But either way she'd call me. She knows I worry; she's good about calling, Harvey."

"Then call her."

Gray nodded, grabbing the wall phone and dialing Lily's cell number. He waited, his distress growing. The doorbell rang, and Harvey

185

went to admit Claudia and the Paluzzis. "We have a little problem," he told them without preamble. "We can't locate the party girl."

Paluzzi muscled his way past him. Gray had hung up the phone, and they met each other halfway across the kitchen. "She's not answering her cell," Gray said shakily.

"Where was she?" Paluzzi asked, reaching for his own cellular. "I'll send a squad car to patrol the area."

"Start with the forest preserve," Gray said. "It's the only unlighted place, the only place that—"

Paluzzi was already speaking into the phone. "She was at the grocery store?" he asked Gray. Gray nodded. Paluzzi spoke some more, and Gray registered the word "Now."

They stood and stared at each other, Paluzzi and Gray, Harvey and Claudia, and Ellen Paluzzi, whose smile had frozen with the news. She still clutched a present with a big pink bow. To Gray it looked obscene.

Finally Claudia stepped forward, reaching for her brother. "I don't believe it, Gray. It's nothing. You'll see." Gray clutched her in his arms.

Paluzzi's cell phone rang. He clicked it on and put it to his ear. "What?" He listened grimly. "Go," he said. "Get backup, and go."

Gray's anguish must have been apparent, because Paluzzi didn't waste time. "They found her car on the side of the forest preserve road. Officer thinks there's a flat."

"Her car?" Gray said. "Not her?"

"She's not in the vehicle."

"Oh, God," Gray said. "He's got her. What if he—"

"The officers will search the area. We'll find her."

Gray closed his eyes and leaned against his sister. "This can't be happening," he said. "It's like last year. Dark and wet and freezing, and Lily alone out there."

He felt Claudia's warm embrace, but he remained cold.

"You know, Lily," Stevens said, almost fondly, "you're much more appealing when you're down on your knees." He touched the buckle of his belt with his left hand; his gun hand was still trained on her.

Lily's fear came up in a sickly rush. He sensed it—she knew he did—and that was what he enjoyed. She needed to be calm; she had to relax. Whatever he made her do, she would be alive, right? And yet a voice inside her said, *No. Die before you submit to him.*

He had worked his zipper all the way down when blue and red lights flashed over them in strobe motion; in one instant she saw his surprise illuminated in crimson. *That's how he'll look in the fires of hell*, she thought bitterly, and it gave her new momentum. The police were there. They would find her car. They would tell Gray and Tony. It was only a matter of time.

He yanked her back up furiously and put the mouth of the pistol against her temple. He whispered into her ear. "If you make a sound, I'll shoot you, and there'll be no second chance this time, Lily. You hear me?"

She nodded, and he drew her backward, deeper into the woods. Lily feared that the crunching of sticks and leaves under their feet was drowned out by the sound of the squawk box in the squad car. She cast desperate glances backward as he dragged her along; she thought she saw the gleam of flashlights. *God*, she thought, *don't let him shoot any more cops.*

Finally he hauled her behind a felled tree. He pushed her down, out of sight, and lay on top of her, his gun against her cheek. "Shh," he said, almost soundlessly. She couldn't see his face in the deeper blackness of the forest, but she felt the pollution of his body against hers. She sensed that he was feeling stress for the first time.

"Get off of me," she whispered.

"Don't struggle," he said in her ear. "You know you mustn't struggle, Cammy. I don't want to hurt you." His hand slid under her jacket and began to pull her shirt out of the waistband of her pants. Lily's terror was momentarily replaced by repulsion. She tried to wriggle away and felt a sudden blow to the side of her head. For a moment she thought she'd been shot again, but he had merely struck her with the pistol. It was enough to make lights dance before her eyes, but not the lights she was desperate to see. She heard nothing, either. No voices, no radio, no footsteps. Despair threatened to overwhelm her, especially when Nob Stevens's hand closed over her naked breast.

"Cammy." His voice floated over her, sinister and sick. "I love you, Cammy."

Lily tasted bile on her tongue. "Cammy is dead," she said out loud.

She must have stunned him, because the blow she expected didn't come. "What?" he asked quietly.

"You had her shot two weeks ago, remember? And today she died. But I'm sure she died inside many times before then, every time you violated her." Tears of anger welled in her eyes. She knew she had to get out from under him, or the pile of mucky leaves they lay in would be her grave. Blood from her head wound trickled into her ear.

"Cammy isn't dead. You're lying." His voice was low and ominous.

"Watch the news and find out," Lily said. "Let me up. I feel like I'm going to throw up. I don't want to throw up on you." She began heaving, and with a disgusted sound and a violent twist of her breast he rolled off of her, then hauled her upright and dragged her farther into the woods, pushing her toward some bushes. "Do it there," he said.

She bent at the waist and clasped her ankles, making dramatic retching sounds. The fingers of her right hand slid inside her sock, where she'd kept a tube of pepper spray for weeks in the event of a surprise attack. She continued gasping as she positioned it in her hand, as she flicked open the catch. Her forefinger slid into the small indentation at the top.

She stood up and spun around, holding her stomach as though she were still nauseous. "I'm sick," she said. His gun was down, but his eyes were wary in the darkness. She stepped closer. "But you're sicker." She lifted her vial and sprayed directly into his eyes.

He screamed in pain, lifting his left hand protectively, instinctively, but, to her horror, raising the gun in his right. He couldn't see her, but his aim was true.

He fired.

TWENTY

PALUZZI ZIPPED THE JACKET he had never taken off. "I'm going to the scene," he said.

Gray was right behind him. "So am I. Don't waste time arguing with me."

Paluzzi said nothing. They ran out together.

In the car Paluzzi got the squad on the radio. "Unit 412, do you read me?" he asked.

For a time they heard only static. Eventually a voice came on. "I read you, sir. We've got men in the woods with flashlights. They're about to come back in; it's a difficult area in the dark, and we're not convinced that she's—hold it, sir, we've got voices, loud voices—we've got a gunshot, sir!"

Gray sat up straight, his body clenched. He stared at the radio as if a close study would bring him the truth.

"Shit," Tony said. "Unit 412!" he yelled into the radio. Then, to Gray, "We're almost there."

Gray knew where they were, but the words were comforting nonetheless. Soon he'd be there, he'd have some control, he'd be able to see things with his own eyes. "Lily had her gun," he said.

Paluzzi said nothing. Gray turned to look at his grim profile and felt a cold burst of fear in his gut. "What? What?"

Paluzzi shook his head. "God, Gray." He was in the forest preserve now. It was dark, very dark, until they turned a bend and saw the lights of the police cars, garish in the night. "They found her gun in the car," Tony said with a quick look of apology. He pulled up behind the squad cars.

Gray could see his Jeep on the road just in front of them. Her phone was there. Her gun was there. Who, then, had fired? He opened his door and swung his feet out of the car. It seemed that every motion cost him huge amounts of energy.

In the woods he saw flickering lights, giant fireflies roaming randomly, up and down, back and forth. They were searching. For what? Bodies? Lily's body? It had been like this the night they'd told him she was shot. He'd been waiting at home, carving a goddamn pumpkin, when the police car pulled into his driveway. The helplessness and the bitter anger of that time returned now at the thought that she might be dead, after all her efforts to avenge one attempt on her life.

He moved forward on rubbery legs, joining Paluzzi, who spoke with an officer. "They're investigating now, sir," the young man was saying.

"Any sign?" Paluzzi said.

"Not yet. We think they're pretty deep in the forest." The young man's face was wooden as his eyes flicked to Gray and then back to Paluzzi.

"So that's it?" Gray asked. "We just stand here while she—"

"They're on it," Paluzzi said.

191

"I'm sorry," Gray started, "I can't just—" He felt suddenly over-whelmed with his misery, his guilt, his fear. "Lily!" he yelled. "Lily! Answer me!" He hurtled into the dark forest, tripping and almost falling over the first root that jutted out of the ground.

He heard Paluzzi coming after him. "Don't be a goddamn idiot," Paluzzi hissed, but Gray ignored him.

He continued to run, calling her name, waiting for some sign, some miracle, just as he had been when the man in blue scrubs, covered with her blood, had come out of surgery and told him that she would proba-bly live. Gray was faster than Paluzzi; sheer desperation gave him speed. He ran blindly, tripping and righting himself, occasionally suffering lashes from branches he didn't see in time. He heard the officers with the flashlights blundering through the underbrush, saw the arc of their lamps as they swung them back and forth. They'd found nothing, he could tell by their urgent searching. One was moving north, another west. Gray moved east.

He slowed to a walk and moved forward silently, concentrating, his eyes adapting to the darkness. He tuned his ears, listening for the smallest sound, for her voice whispering anything at all.

What he heard, finally, was a sort of gasping. He stopped and heard it again. He wasn't sure if it was a soft crying, the hissing of an animal, or perhaps—he fought the image even as it came to him—the sound of dying.

He followed it. He was close now, so close that he slowed his pace, afraid of what he would find. He inched through piles of wet leaves, shivering with cold and dread.

He cried out in terror when a hand closed around his ankle.

———

Lily knew she was hit. She felt the pain in her shoulder, the burning, and she felt the trickle of warm blood down her chest, down over the

192

scar he'd left her before. She dropped instinctively to her belly and used her good arm to inch away. She was furious, and glad to be. It filled her with energy.

She could hear him panting, gasping with the pain in his eyes. She had blinded him for the moment, and that was all she needed. The police had heard the gunfire. As always, she would rely on the police.

Nob fired again. He was swearing bitterly, calling her every name he could summon while his eyes burned in his head. Lily knew all of this without looking at him, and she dragged herself, trying not to think of her wound, of the blood she was trailing along the leaves. The tree trunks creaked and cracked as they swayed in the wind. A sound like water reached her, and she wondered if she were near a creek; then she realized it was the sighing of the trees as they met and rubbed together high above her.

She heard Gray's voice and froze. Gray. What was he doing here? He'd be in danger. He had no weapon, and he was too emotional; she could hear the fear and worry in his tone. She wanted to call to him, to tell him to go back, but she couldn't. She felt a sudden agony that had nothing to do with her bullet wound. Her husband was walking toward Nob Stevens, and Nob no longer had anything to lose.

She tried to move faster without alerting Stevens to her presence. If she could get far enough away, she could call to Gray without giving the governor another chance at retaliation. She concentrated on motion. The leaves smelled dank and felt cold, and occasionally sharp things penetrated the skin of her palm; she would reach down and pull them out, then keep on. Gray's voice continued calling her; she felt tears of frustration running down her face. She wanted to go to him, to calm his fears. His pain was hers; she understood that he feared she was dead. After all he'd gone through before, the time when her prognosis was uncertain and then her long journey back, he didn't deserve even a moment of despair.

He was coming closer; would he reach her first, or would Stevens find him? For a time she heard nothing. She'd put a fair distance between herself and her enemy. She was beginning to think that Gray had gone back the way he had come. A part of her felt desolate at the possibility. He would be safer, though, much safer, back at the road. *Let the police handle it, Gray*, she thought. She willed him to turn back.

As she tried to ease herself into a sitting position, she heard Gray, distantly, cry out in surprise. She stared into the intense darkness, trying to see, to smell, to feel anything to determine what was happening. Then, with a sickly comprehension, she heard Nob Stevens's voice, still in pain but triumphant nevertheless. "Lily! Oh, Lily! I've got your husband."

God, she thought. *No.*

"I've got my gun to his head, Lily. I can't see, but I can feel. Do you want to risk it, or do you want to show yourself?"

He was about one hundred feet from her. She eased closer, gauging his position. The men with the flashlights, having heard his voice, were coming closer, calling out to each other. The occasional illumination helped Lily to observe the scene. She saw Gray, standing irresolute. *Don't run*, she thought. *Don't run.* Nob Stevens, as he'd promised, held a gun near Gray's temple. They were in a tiny clearing, near a large black thing that was probably a fallen tree. Stevens's eyes, which she had glimpsed in the torch beam, were streaming water and tightly shut. Even bleeding, she had an advantage over him. He was blind, but he wouldn't be much longer.

She crept nearer, easing up into a squat. She didn't want to reveal her location by calling out, but if she didn't say something, she risked Gray's life. The police were coming closer. Lily knew Nob Stevens. If he was going to be apprehended, he wanted to kill her first. If he needed to kill her husband to draw her out, he would do so. She moved closer, torn by indecision.

Stevens decided for her. "You have five seconds to answer me, Lily, and then he dies. One."

Swearing under her breath and nearly closing the distance between them, Lily saw her chance. He was in front of the fallen tree.

"Two. Lily, I thought you cared for him more."

"Maybe you killed her," Gray said, angry. "And if you did, you son of a bitch, I'll—"

"Shut up," said Stevens, waving the gun near Gray's head. "Three, Lily."

With a lunge that shot pain throughout her body, Lily catapulted from her hiding place; she saw that Gray had moved at the same time, catching Stevens's gun hand and grappling with him. They sounded like gladiators, grunting and cursing. Lily, airborne, caught Nob Stevens at the waist, pushing backward with all the aggression of an offensive lineman. His calves hit the fallen tree and he went backward, his gun firing into the sky before Gray kicked it out of his hand. She thought at first that Gray had missed, but then she realized he was just kicking, perhaps to subdue the prone Stevens, but more likely for other reasons. Lily sprayed Stevens again, and he screamed as the pepper hit his closed eyes.

"Gray, stop," she said, but not to protect Stevens. Gray eventually halted and turned to her, wiping sweat from his face, but she was on Stevens now, punching, clawing, kicking, hurting. She went for his vulnerable places, and his grunts and cries of pain did not deter her. *I'm not back on the force yet*, she thought. *I don't have to be ethical.* Every time she landed a blow, she thought of someone he'd hurt. *Camilla. Emily. Danny. Gray. Me. Linda. Joshua.*

Hands were pulling at her, pulling her away. She felt herself losing consciousness even as she lost her grip on Nob Stevens. *It was worth it*, she thought. *They can arrest me, even throw me in jail. It was worth it.*

There seemed to be voices everywhere. The men with flashlights. Tony? And Gray—Gray was alive, she hadn't let him down the way she'd let down Danny. She'd wanted her hands on Nob Stevens ever since then, and she'd finally had her way. She was floating now, floating backward until all she saw were the sighing trees, their top branches spiderfine and swaying against the black sky and, beyond, the stars.

The last thing she heard was Gray saying, "God, she's bleeding! He shot her again!" Then the darkness closed in.

When she woke, Lily was in a room she didn't recognize. She heard something, some sort of din, someone yelling. She turned, groggily, looking for the source. What she saw was Gray. His face was near, concerned and loving. She wanted to touch him, but when she moved, it hurt, so she lay still. "Gray," she croaked.

He held up a glass of water. It was a hospital cup; she recognized the type from her previous stay. She took a sip, then another, and looked around. Oh yes, she was back in the hospital. "Are you all right?" she asked.

He laughed. "Lily, if I didn't think you loved me, I certainly would know it now. You were shot, Lily, and beaten. God only knows what he—"

"I'm okay," she said.

Gray looked unconvinced. "You didn't need surgery this time. It grazed your shoulder. It's going to leave another scar, though."

Suddenly Lily remembered, with a horrible weight of guilt. "God, the baby. Did I lose the baby? Gray, did I—"

"The baby is all right," he said. "It must be tough like you. Tough as a nut, and just as small right now." He placed a protective hand on her abdomen. "Lily," he said wearily, rubbing her gently. "Don't get shot anymore."

"Stevens," she said.

"He's in custody. The whole world is waiting to hear what he has to say for himself. He's got a lawyer, and he seems ready to tough it out. He doesn't look so good, though. You blacked his eye, Lily, and you broke his nose."

She lay back, nodding. "Good."

Gray frowned. "I wish you had let me do it."

Lily shrugged. "As I recall, you were able to contribute. What's all that noise?"

"Reporters outside. They want you bad. The cop who wouldn't die. You solved a seventeen-year-old murder and, well, crimes that go back a lot further than that. You've kept a low profile, and now they all want you. They must hate Claudia for that one-on-one she got with you."

"She'll get a lot more. I'm not interested in talking to anyone else. And she understands, because she was in it with us."

"Right." Gray seemed suddenly ill at ease. "Do you want some rest? I can go in the corner and—"

"You should go home."

"That's not going to happen." He stood at her side, solid and determined.

Lily looked at him. Her eyes felt so dry they were painful; she was almost relieved by the lubricating tears that filled them. "Gray, I was coming for you. I wasn't going to let him shoot you. I couldn't let him know my position." She could hear the pleading in her own voice, but for what she wasn't sure. Understanding? Forgiveness?

Gray's face reflected neither; it showed compassion. "Babe," he said, "I wasn't putting that sort of responsibility on you. We both jumped him on the count of three. But you saved me, Lily. You lunged out of nowhere, and even in the dark I could see that you were hurt, that you were bleeding. You are a hero, and you've never been anything but a hero to me."

"A hero," she said, trying out the word.

"Get used to it. The accolades will be flowing in for a long time. Lots of tributes, pomp and circumstance. Maybe a parade or two."

She laughed, but she stopped when she saw he wasn't joking. "I don't want that," she said. "I want us to go home."

She reached for his hand, and he gripped hers tightly. "I'll take you home just as soon as I can," he said. "Listen, there are some people here—remember our party? I know it's hard to believe it was just last night. They're out there—Claudia and Harvey, Tony and Ellen. Your mom. And my brothers and parents are on their way."

"All the way from Maine?" she asked.

"They want to be here for you. They all want to be here for you."

Lily thought about that, and then she smiled. "I want to see my mom," she said. "Send her in first. I want to tell her about the baby."

TWENTY-ONE

Sergeant Lily Caldwell of the Capitol City Police Department got home later than expected. She'd been on "cutie duty" ever since her pregnancy had become visible. She'd despised Tony at first for making her the ambassador to the grade schools, telling kids to say no to drugs and to trust their local police officers. After a few weeks of the job, however, she'd realized that she loved it—that she was, in fact, good at it. The children were fascinated by her, since the majority of them usually knew who she was. They'd seen her on the television news or on the talk shows or in the magazine and newspaper articles. She was a celebrity, and not just in Capitol City.

When she'd returned from maternity leave, she'd asked for a shorter schedule, and she told Tony she wanted to keep cutie duty. He'd agreed wholeheartedly. Tony was somehow afraid that she was a magnet for trouble, she knew, and he felt far too fatherly toward her to treat her with the same detachment with which he treated other officers. Lily had come to accept that, even to like it a little.

Now she was home, shivering in the autumn wind. It was November. More than a year had passed since her last encounter with Nob Stevens, and much had happened to keep her mind off of that particular person. But Lily had been reminded of him in many ways. For one, his court date for the murder of Camilla kept getting postponed; he hadn't been charged with the murders of Emily or Danny, because the police didn't have enough evidence to link him to the crimes. They did, however, have the accomplices Stevens worked with in the murder of Camilla Martin and the assault on Joshua Randall. Another reminder came when Stevens's lawyer made public statements about his client being "misunderstood," another when Linda Stevens had quietly obtained her divorce and just as quietly remarried, and yet another when George Martin made his tearful statement to the press, explaining his wife's difficult childhood and her grateful escape into George's friendship and love. He spoke of his daughter, Emily, and how she had learned of her real father's existence when she got into a discussion with a biology teacher, a colleague of hers at Nazareth High School, and found that her mother and father, with their blood types, could not have parented her. Camilla had begged her to leave the truth in the past, where it needed to stay, but Emily had been a curious girl. She had begun to investigate. No one else, not even George Martin, knew exactly what had happened next.

Overwhelmed by these thoughts, Lily ran up the steps of her home to relieve her mother of the baby, only to find Gray at the door.

"Hi, beautiful," he said, taking her jacket.

"What's wrong?" Lily asked, looking around. "Where's Mom?"

"She went home. She has a date, and she was glad to see me here a little early today."

"A date, huh?" Lily said absently. "That's nice. Where's Julia?"

"Sleeping." A soft cry emanated from a back room, and Lily brightened.

Gray laughed. "Not anymore." He left the room briefly and returned with a little dark-haired baby tucked into his arm. "There's Mama," he said as the baby reached for Lily. "You want Mama?"

Lily took her gratefully. After several hours away she was as ready to nurse as her daughter was. "There's my angel," she crooned, taking the tiny girl to an easy chair. The baby gasped with eagerness, her dark eyes staring expectantly at Lily's breasts as Lily worked to open her nursing bra.

Lily laughed merrily as the baby latched on, and the infant's tiny hand began to trace her mother's scar, something with which she had lately become fascinated. Settled, relieved, content, Lily looked up at Gray, who smiled at both of them.

"I love you," she said.

"I know," he told her. "I love you, too. And that little girl there."

Lily smiled, leaned her head against the chair, and looked out the window. Her eyes became distant as she watched leaves skitter past the pane. The sky was gray, but a brightness shone through it. "His book comes out today."

Gray sighed. "I know."

"It will sell. Everyone wants to read it, to know why someone does those things. They want explanations for something there is no explanation for. He's a mutation."

"Now you're talking like a scientist."

"I'm married to one. It rubs off." She gave him another smile. She was doing more smiling these days. It was impossible not to feel joyful with a baby in the house, impossible not to feel happy to be back with her husband. Her attempts at forgiveness, while difficult at first, had reaped more rewards than Lily could have hoped. She was on better terms with Tony, with her mother, with Gray. She'd been able to accept a new image of Danny, one in which he wasn't quite so saintly. If he'd lived, she would have had it out with him, yelled at him, punched him in the arm. Instead, she'd told him in her prayers that she forgave him, just as she expected him to forgive her. All of these efforts of spirit had brought her a new maturity.

But there was a lasting bitterness in her heart, and the name of Nob Stevens still made her feel hot with the desire for revenge.

"I spoke to a group of high school kids today. Not normally my age group, but Tony arranged it. The school requested me."

"Your reputation precedes you," Gray said, stroking Lily's hair, then moving his finger down to touch the translucent skin of Julia's pudgy cheek. The baby had eyes only for her mother as she clutched the breast contentedly, making little sucking sounds and occasionally smiling, letting pale milk dribble across her face.

"I was waiting in the hall, waiting for this English class to be over. They were reading *Macbeth*," Lily said. "I didn't remember it at all, but in the end Macbeth is killed. Slain. By Macduff. Macbeth killed Macduff's whole family, even his children." She looked down at her baby, and her arms tightened. "So Macduff killed Macbeth, who was under the impression that he couldn't be killed."

"Surprise," Gray said.

"Yeah. And then he puts Macbeth's head on a pole for everyone to see. And everyone is cheering. Death to the tyrant. He was hated, because he was hateful. He deserved to have his head on a pole."

"No doubt."

"And Nob Stevens." Lily squinted with the effort of trying to put her feelings into words. "He's written a book. I won't read it, Gray. I know it will be self-serving and horrible, that he will suggest that nothing was his fault, that it was out of his control. He'll probably blame me, like he did that night—"

"Don't." Gray touched her hand. "Don't, Lily. Don't go back. You suffered for a long time, and you emerged victorious. Now you have a new baby and a new career and a husband who loves you more than anyone in the world . . ."

Lily looked into his gray eyes; she was on the verge of tears, but not tearful. Gray was right—of course he was right—but it hurt; it burned inside her like the pain of labor. It was hard to relinquish the hate.

Their door flew open and Harvey bustled in, Claudia in his wake. "Hello, family!" he said heartily. "Nice boob, Lily."

"Thanks," she said, grinning. Harvey always cheered her up with his obnoxious humor. "How was the honeymoon?"

"Wonderful," Claudia said, looking at her new husband. "Very romantic."

"What she means," Harvey said, pulling Claudia against him, "is that we had sex almost constantly."

Claudia rolled her eyes but didn't struggle in his arms. "Men and women have such different interpretations of—"

"Sex," Harvey said mildly, kissing her.

Gray stood up. "Could you not talk about ravaging my sister until I'm out of the room?" he asked good-naturedly. "I prefer to think of you two as having a platonic relationship."

"Yeah, okay," Harvey said, placing his hands firmly on Claudia's bottom. "So are you doing okay, Lily?"

Lily knew what he meant. "Did you guys get a copy?"

Claudia nodded solemnly. "This morning. At the airport. I have to read it, Lily, for my job. I have to know what he—"

"That's okay," Lily said. "I'll want the abridged version. You can fill me in on the main points. Gray has made me promise not to read anything about it. Believe it or not, I don't even know what they're finally calling it." She went for a casual tone. "So what *is* the title of this noble tome?"

Claudia and Harvey exchanged a glance. "You're going to hear it on television anyway—"

"Go ahead, I can take it," Lily said, stroking her daughter's thistle-down hair, then switching her to nurse on the other side.

"Stop staring at Lily's breasts, Harvey," Gray said.

"Sorry. I don't suppose I could expose Claudia's?"

Lily laughed, covering herself with a blanket. She knew Harvey was trying to distract her from the pain she was about to feel. "Just tell me the title, already."

"*The Burden of Greatness*," Claudia said. She looked apologetic. "It's already on the bestseller list."

Lily nodded. She felt the tightening in her gut, but she tried to hide it. "That's appropriately pompous."

Gray wasn't fooled. "Let it go, babe. Your life will be so much happier if you let it go. He'll die in prison. They won't let him see a dime of the profits."

"But some people will be impressed. He'll be a celebrity, Gray. A celebrity. They make these people with no morality, no feelings, into heroes. Charles Manson has fans. Nob Stevens will have fans."

"You're a much bigger hero, Lily," Claudia insisted. "And I happen to know you've received many book offers."

Lily sighed, suddenly exhausted. "I don't have time for that. I don't have time—"

"You're feeling the burden of greatness, aren't you?" quipped Harvey, his hands slipping thoughtfully up Claudia's back and into her hair.

Lily laughed again. "Harvey, you'll be good for me. I'm glad you guys are home. We missed you when you were in Hawaii. Nice tans, by the way."

Claudia noticed that Julia had finished nursing and was merely playing with Lily's bra. "Can I have her, Lily?"

Lily sat the baby up. Julia belched delicately, then smiled widely at everyone, displaying pink gums. Lily offered her to Claudia.

"Come to your aunt, you precious baby," Claudia crooned, swinging Julia through the air before settling her against her chest.

Harvey smiled at her.

"You look good as a mommy," he said. "If I did my work properly, maybe you will be soon."

Gray slapped Harvey's back. "You're obsessed with sex, my friend."

"It's a delightful obsession," Harvey said. "What's to drink around here?"

Gray led his friend from the room. They talked animatedly, like boys in college again.

Lily observed Claudia and her daughter. "Can you stay for dinner?" she asked. "We'd love to hear your honeymoon stories."

Claudia nodded. "We'd like that. You guys are our best friends, you know. It's so nice to have another happy couple to talk to and to double-date with. And obviously Harvey needs to talk about sex with someone other than me."

"Fine with me," Lily said.

Claudia kissed the baby's head. "Do you find it—is it harder to, uh, get personal time, now that you have Julia?"

Lily shrugged. "Not really. She sleeps pretty well now. Things can't always take as long as they once did, but there's always time for *something*." She smiled mischievously at Claudia. "We're becoming very creative at finding those times."

"Hmm. Sounds fun," Claudia said. "I want a baby, Lily. I hope I can give Harvey one. Or more than one."

"You love him a lot."

"Yeah." Claudia smiled. "He sort of tricked me into it, and then there I was."

"Love is like that," Lily said, smiling at Julia, who gave her another toothless grin in return. Still smiling, Lily asked, "When do they move him? For his trial?"

Claudia didn't pretend not to know who Lily referred to, despite the sudden subject change. "On Friday, I think. They're taking him to a secure location; that's all they'll say about the change of venue. Apparently they feel he'll get a fairer trial there."

"Like it will be fair anywhere," Lily said. "The guy's on the best-seller list, you just told me, and—"

"We'll wait and see, Lily. Come on, don't let it get to you. Don't let him win. He's in a cage, and you're free."

Lily nodded. "I know. I know. But every once in a while, it feels like it's the other way around."

TWENTY-TWO

ON FRIDAY, NOVEMBER 17, Capitol City, along with much of America, waited in front of the television to see live coverage of Nob Stevens's transfer out of the Capitol City jail. Nob Stevens had not been seen publicly since his last appearance as governor, which had been the press conference announcing his candidacy for re-election. Lily noted the stunned silence of the little crowd outside the courthouse where Stevens waited with county guards.

Nob Stevens, in prison orange and bulky chains, suddenly looked his age. His hair, once expensively treated to look just on the verge of silver, was now almost white. Lily resented it, somehow. It gave him the appearance of a sage or a prophet, and he seemed to play that up with the wise look he sent to the cameras. "Asshole," she said as Nob shuffled along, milking sympathy by holding up his manacles with a rueful expression.

The guards stopped Nob briefly, saying something to him that no one could hear. The cameraman for Channel Seven took the opportunity to pan the small crowd; it was made up of reporters, police officials, and additional security officers. Tony was there. Lily didn't see Linda Stevens in the crowd. The woman had seemed far too dignified to be a part of a little circus like this; besides, she was Linda Randall now.

Linda had written a letter to Lily, thanking her for all she'd done, for being brave, for pursuing justice, for saving Joshua Randall and Linda herself, and for telling her to get angry. "The more I thought about those words," Linda had written, "the more I felt able to resurrect the woman I once was, the one who had spirit and spunk, like you do, Lily."

Lily had been flattered by the letter and moved by Linda's effort to write it. She hadn't been obligated to acknowledge Lily in any way, and a different sort of woman might have chosen to resent the police officer who had exposed her husband. Lily wrote back to Linda when she heard about her marriage to Josh Randall, congratulating her and assuring her that the admiration was mutual.

Lily thought of this as she watched the little crowd that hunched into their coats on this particularly cold November day, watching Nob Stevens hobbling along and doing his absurd dance of self-pity. Suddenly she sat on the edge of the couch. "Gray," she said. He was going through a file that he'd brought home from the office, his glasses perched on his nose. "Gray, look!"

He looked up absently and said, "Hmm?"

Lily gripped the couch cushions. "Damn, the camera moved away. I recognized someone. I thought it was—"

The camera was again on Nob Stevens, but someone jostled the videographer, and his focus moved slightly to the left, where a man emerged from the crowd, a man in a nondescript security uniform. "Oh, God," Lily said. "That's George Martin!"

Martin was smiling slightly, waiting for Stevens to come past. His hand was in his pocket. "How did he get through security?" Lily asked.

"God, I need to call Tony on his cell. How come no one recognizes him?"

But she knew why, even as she asked the question. He looked like a hollow shell of the man she'd seen on television a year before. This man looked ten years older and embittered by life. Even his smile seemed more like a mask of anguish. Gray handed her the phone, and she began to dial with trembling fingers, realizing at the same time that it was too late and seeing the scene, which America would only understand moments later, as if in slow motion: Nob Stevens came close enough to George Martin to recognize who he was. Martin smiled, and Stevens raised his eyebrows, then looked uncertainly at his guards and started to say something—but Martin had fired his weapon through his pocket. The security men who saw Nob fall weren't even sure where the bullet came from, and a moment of chaos occurred, a moment captured before the camera was turned off and Channel Seven switched to an emergency news report screen. In that final image of cops and bodyguards scanning the crowd and yelling over each other in a panic of indecision, Lily focused on George Martin, who bent over Nob Stevens with a smug expression and said something to him, even as Nob writhed on the ground, even as someone ripped at his orange shirt and tried to assess the damage.

Lily read his lips, had known what he would say anyway, and she felt a mixture of revulsion and grim satisfaction at the words: "That was for Camilla."

"Stevens was alive when they put him in the ambulance," Tony told her moments later on his cell phone. "That's all I know. I need to find out how these fuckers let George Martin walk in and pose as a goddamn—"

Someone interrupted him, and Lily listened to the muffled sound of his voice as he consulted with someone nearby.

"Bullshit," she heard Tony say, and then he was back. "It was his brother, Lil. George Martin had a brother who planned it with him. The brother got the security job months ago, then said his brother would fill in for him today, that his brother had security experience. I don't know. I've got to get the whole story. They've both been arrested. Dammit," Tony said, frustrated. "Why do these people bring this crap on themselves?"

Lily knew why. She thought of George's face the moment before he pulled the trigger: bitter, hardened like petrified wood, and then showing the brief release, the wild look of euphoria as he spoke to the suffering Stevens on the ground. George Martin had been living for that moment, and now that it was over, he would probably go back to feeling dead.

———————

Two days later several notable things happened in the life of Lily Caldwell. First, her daughter, Julia, revealed her first tooth. Lily tapped it with a tiny spoon to prove it to Gray, who said he didn't see it. The spoon rang like a minuscule bell, and mother and father exchanged joyful looks. "A tooth," Gray said wonderingly. "Before I know it, she'll be dating."

Lily laughed, stroking the baby's hair. "I think you'll have some time to adjust," she said, continuing to feed Julia her bananas.

"She looks so much like you, Lily," Gray said, kissing both of his girls. "I couldn't have wished for a more beautiful daughter."

"What a nice compliment for us both," Lily said, placid and content. "And you're pretty nice, too, for a boy."

Gray laughed, taking the spoon from her. "I'll feed her; you go catch up on your work."

Lily was working on a booklet to give to the children she visited while on cutie duty. It detailed the roles of the police officer, what children should do when they met strangers, how children should react if they saw stray animals, and other things she often mentioned when she spoke to little ones.

Freed from mother duty, she returned to Gray's laptop. She went on the Internet, as she'd been doing hourly ever since Stevens had been shot, and she saw the headline "Indicted Governor Dies of Gunshot Wound." She stared at it for a full minute, not even bothering to read the story. A photo of Nob Stevens was there by the headline, a photo of him as he'd once been rather than one of the man he'd become. *Why is that?* she wondered. *Whose editorial decision was it to post a photo of Stevens before his fall?* He looked handsome, confident, well-coiffed. He stared into the camera with a bold expression, one that projected both self-assurance and intimidation.

Lily felt a familiar fluttering in her stomach—something between fear and hatred.

"Gray," she said softly. "Gray!"

"Huh?" he called from the kitchen.

"He's dead."

Gray appeared in the doorway. "Stevens?"

Lily scanned the article. "It says he underwent several surgeries to repair his stomach. Excruciating pain. Blah, blah, blah."

She was surprised to realize that she felt nothing—certainly not regret, but not bitter satisfaction, either. She didn't want to dance and sing, "Ding-dong, Nob Stevens is dead," and she didn't feel like crowing about his painful demise.

"You okay?" Gray asked, peering once over his shoulder to check on the baby.

"I am. I guess I didn't need his head on a pole after all, though. This doesn't mean much to me, when all is said and done."

"He has to face them now, Lily. The people he killed. His sister, his daughter. Danny. He has to explain it all to God."

Lily said tonelessly, "I'm sure he'll assume God has read his book."

Gray studied her carefully. "You're okay? Let me get the baby, and we'll come and cuddle with you."

Lily smiled at the doorway where he'd been. Gray was good. Gray kept her healthy, kept her sane. And Julia gave her a future to believe in; all of the children she worked with were the future.

She clicked the Nob Stevens headline away and went back to the document she'd been composing. She needed to ask Tony what he thought of it, but she wanted to incorporate some information about abuse, rape, incest. The children were young, and of course she couldn't use those terms, but they all needed to know that they were strong, that they were important, and that they didn't have to be victimized by any monsters who might loom over them in the path of life. They should know that even though they were good and the world cared about them, there were people out there who didn't do as they should: bad parents, bad teachers, bad leaders, bad cops.

How old did they have to be, Lily wondered, before they heard that message? How old did they have to be before they were told that they must value themselves, even when others didn't value them?

She had just begun to type when Gray and the baby came to sit with her. Julia's hair was damp; Gray had obviously wiped some food out of it while he'd been cleaning her little face. He was very efficient that way. "Ma," Julia said, aiming a tiny finger at Lily even while her legs clung, monkey-like, to Gray.

"Yes. Ma." Lily beamed at her baby and put her work aside.

———

The third significant event was a phone call from Linda Randall. She asked for Lily, and Lily didn't realize at first who she was. Julia was happily babbling in her ear, and Lily, distracted, handed her to Gray.

"I'm sorry, who is this?" she asked.

"Linda Randall. I met you at the hospital, and—"

"Oh, Mrs. Randall, I'm so sorry. My daughter was yelling in my ear."

"She sounds very happy."

"She is," Lily said. Then, after some hesitation, "I hope you are, too."

"I am, Lily. I am surprisingly happy, given the bizarre changes in my life over the span of a year."

"I'm sorry that, uh—your ex-husband had to suffer."

She sniffed. "I imagine you're not sure how you feel, and neither am I. But that's not why I'm calling. I spoke today with Claudia Caldwell. She wanted a comment about a story she's doing regarding Nob's death. I gave her one, because I trust her. I have watched how careful, how dignified, she has been with the story as it emerged, how well she dealt with you when you were obviously not thrilled about giving an interview."

"Claudia is a true professional. And I don't say that because she is related to me."

"I agree with you. I asked Claudia, while I was on the phone with her, if she would be willing to come and have lunch with me someday. I'd like you to be there, as well."

"Lunch?" Lily asked. "That's very nice. Is there some reason—"

Linda Randall laughed. "I've been very shy of people, Lily, since Nob was arrested. At best they are curious, and at worst they somehow think I am implicated by his crimes. I've sequestered myself from humanity, except from my husband. Josh has been a godsend. He understands the pain, and he actually brings joy, even humor, into my life."

"I know what you mean. Without Gray—well, I was without him for a while, and it was the hardest part of the entire ordeal."

"So you see, you understand that, too. I've decided to begin letting the world in again, but I'm being very selective. I'm not ready for people who don't understand, only for people who do. You and Claudia are women I admire, women who see this for what it is."

"Mrs. Randall, I—"

"Linda, please. Call me Linda."

"Linda. I would love to have lunch with you."

"I'm not living in splendid quarters. We live in a modest house behind Josh's studio."

Lily laughed. "Do I strike you as a 'splendid quarters' sort of person?"

Linda's laugh was surprisingly girlish. "No. That's why I like you, Lily. You've helped me so much, you can't even know."

"You know, there's something you can do to help me, too."

"Really?"

"I suppose we can talk more about this at lunch. I'm trying to compose a program for children. Sort of a cross between a self-esteem session and a hidden warning about the perils of the world. You'd be a wonderful source, as a former first lady. As I recall, you did a lot of charity work for children's causes."

"I did. I met many children along the way. And I'll be a mother soon, so your idea is very important to me."

"Congratulations!" Lily cried.

"Thank you," said Linda. "I thought it was an unattainable dream. I think that's the main thing children should know: dreams can come true."

"I can't agree more," Lily said. "And we should find a way to incorporate parents into the program. To ask for their vigilance as well." Lily had a sudden image of Fred pushing her down and of her mother clutching a spatula, looking wide-eyed and lost.

"So you'll come to lunch? Next Saturday, maybe?"

"I'll be there," Lily said. She hung up the phone and closed her eyes, slightly overwhelmed by the events of the day. Then she opened her eyes and dialed again before she could change her mind.

"Hello?" said her mother.

"Hi, Mom. I wanted to call and say thanks."

Her mother was surprised. "Thanks for what, honey?"

"For watching Julia for us, and for being a good mom."

"Oh, honey, you know I love to watch the baby. It's no trouble at all."

"But I've been trouble to you. Ever since Fred I've been hard on you. It wasn't fair. I'm sorry," Lily said. It was the most specific she'd ever been when discussing her rape with her mother.

"Lily—oh, Lily. You were suffering. I should have known. I should have done something. I should have—"

"You did fine, Mom. You were a good mother, and I blamed you for what he did, and it wasn't right. I don't blame you anymore." She could hear her mother's tears, soft and muffled, and it filled her with elation. "I love you, Mom."

"Oh, Lily," her mother said.

"Mom, it's okay. Do you need a minute? To go compose yourself or something? I could hang up—"

"No, no," her mother said. "I'm fine."

"All right." Lily looked at her lap, uncertain now what to say. The apology was over, but she was unpracticed in the everyday conversations of women. She took a stab at it. "So, this guy you're dating. What's he like?" she asked.

Her mother sighed. "Oh, Lily, you've grown so much; you've changed so much. I'm so proud of you."

"Okay," Lily said uncomfortably. "Thanks. So what's this guy's name?"

"His name is Wallace. He works with me at the bookstore."

"Wallace? Is he cute?"

"Well . . . yes, for an older man."

"Older? How old is he?" asked Lily, starting to enjoy herself. It wasn't different, in many ways, from interrogating a suspect.

"Oh, I imagine he's in his late fifties. A bit older than I am."

"Is he single?"

"Lily. Of course he is. He's a widower."

"And where did he take you when you went out?"

"We went to a film and to a late dinner."

"Did he expect anything from you? He wasn't one of those guys, was he?"

"Oh, no, honey, I'm a very slow mover," her mother said. "We're just dating is all."

"Hmm."

They talked some more, about Wallace, and her mother's job, and Lily's job, and babies, and Lily found that she'd talked to her mother on the telephone for half an hour; she'd never done that, not since she'd left home. It felt good and right, and Lily decided that she was simply a late bloomer, in almost everything. If it took her until she was thirty-two to realize what it was to be a daughter, a mother, a wife, then so be it.

She was learning, and she was trying.

EPILOGUE

LILY AND GRAY WATCHED their daughter as she slept in her crib: her arms flung above her head with the abandon of exhaustion, her lips still pursed from nursing, her lashes dark and lovely against her pale, chubby cheeks. "She's the antidote," Lily said. "For all the pain."

"And you have unlimited dosage," her husband said.

In bed Lily snuggled up to Gray and smiled sleepily when his hands wandered predictably over her body. "Were you looking to do some scientific research again?" she asked.

"It's an ongoing project," he said in her ear.

"When do you think you'll have the results?" she asked.

"Mmm. This sort of thing, it's not over for years. The data keeps changing, and the results become skewed. And then you have to start over, testing the variables."

"Long-term?" she asked, smiling.

"Till death do us part," he told her, pressing his lips to hers.

The End

ACKNOWLEDGMENTS

To those who helped me in my research, I am grateful, especially to the following people: Officer Kevin James Connolly of the NEIU Police, for his good-natured willingness to answer a host of bizarre questions; to the librarians at Trinity High School, especially Sue Tindall, for her help with DNA research; and to my late colleague Paulette Nelson, for her answers to my questions about biology and blood type. Any mistakes within are undoubtedly mine rather than theirs.

Many thanks go to my wonderful agent, Kristin Lindstrom, who believed in my work when others did not, and who stood by me on the rocky road to publication. Agents like her are few and far between, and I know how lucky I am.

To the people who read and critiqued my manuscript: Karen Osborne, Kathi Baron, Martha Whitehead, Lenora Rand, Cynthia Quam, Kae Penner-Howell, Jeff Buckley, Katherine Rohaly, Claudia Rohaly, Kevin Connolly, Linda Rohaly, and William E. Rohaly.

Thanks to Karen Osborne, as well, for all of her generous PR efforts on my behalf and her willingness to share her substantial knowledge of the publishing industry.

Thanks to my brother Bill Rohaly and to his wife, Ann Rohaly, for their help. To all of my siblings—Bill, Claudia, Linda, Christopher, and his wife, Cindy—for their support. In addition I wish to thank all of my relatives, especially my late Aunt Barbara Rohaly and my niece Mary Katherine, for their encouragement of my writing.

To my colleagues at Trinity High School, especially the members of the English Department, who are particularly supportive: Rose Crnkovich, Linda Harrington, Cynthia Ellis, Sheila Scott, and John Allen.

My thanks to Kristina Sado, a very patient and talented photographer. Thanks to Laura at the Elmhurst College reference desk for her online research help. Thanks to Lisa and Burt Blanchard, who were always helpful in computer emergencies. Thanks to Mark and Ann Marie Andersen, my first webfans. Thanks to Lydia Brauer, who will one day lead seminars.

Thank you to my contacts at Midnight Ink, who were both friendly and professional: Barbara Moore, Kevin Brown, Wade Ostrowski, and Brian Farrey.

I wish to thank Jeff Buckley for reading endless drafts of manuscripts and encouraging me when I had lost enthusiasm. Thanks also to Ian and Graham Buckley, who put up with my hours on the computer without too many complaints.

Finally, thank you to the great Mary Stewart, my favorite author, whose novels I have read and reread and whose work inspired me to try to write a novel of my own.

Read on for an excerpt from the
first Madeline Mann mystery by Julia Buckley

Pity Him Afterwards

COMING SOON FROM MIDNIGHT INK

ONE

My capricious episodes have made me notorious in my family. Often unexpected, even by me, they are whimsical impulses I sometimes feel compelled to follow. Often my motivation is clear—as in the doll-head-shaving incident when I was seven, prompted by my older brother's comment that my Beautiful Chrissy was "too girlie"—but sometimes the notion is a bit more mysterious, like the infamous wild ride I took in my father's gray Celebrity when I was seventeen. I'd been a sedate driver previous to the incident and have been ever since, but on this afternoon some demon caused me to rocket down Alder, Webley's quietest side street. I shot past a playground, glimpsed the pale, shocked faces of an elderly hand-holding couple in matching sweatsuits, and set some aged doggies to barking. Despite some passionate last-minute braking, I rear-ended a newly minted Mr. Whippy ice-cream truck and consequently alienated my dear father for a full month.

These sorts of occurrences earned me a nickname from both of my brothers: Madman. It wasn't a clever creation on their part, since it's merely an ironic combination of my first and last names, Madeline

Mann, but I have a feeling Madman would have become my nickname even if I'd been christened Jill Smith. Though I'm basically a quiet, thoughtful person, I can sometimes be ruled by my impulses—based upon what I like to call the "floating vibes" I feel in a given situation. Sometimes I need to take vibe-restoring action. It's hard to explain, but there's a certain rightness about it within me. It's the only way to begin this story, I've decided, because I never would have become involved in a murder investigation if I hadn't, in fact, been mutinously reacting to something else.

A case in point is my hair. Jack, my upstairs neighbor for two years and my boyfriend for one, loved my brunette locks; they were fairly thick and smooth and were worn straight and simple to my shoulders. When Jack and I had our first big argument one autumn night and I stormed out of his apartment and flew down the stairs to mine, I was definitely in one of those unstable moods. I felt it was over, and I felt it was Jack's fault. I was miserable, but furious.

Who knows where wacky ideas come from? I simply had one. I took out my barber's shears and carefully cut off two or three inches of my hair. I ran out to the drugstore and bought L'Oréal Preference blonde dye—"Because I'm worth it," I murmured throatily to myself in the store aisle. I hurried home and applied the smelly stuff without further thought. I had to let it sit for forty-five minutes, during which time I played Peter, Paul, and Mary's *Ten Years Together* CD and sang along with every song while I perused a *Cat Fancy* magazine. (I don't have cats, but I fancy them. My landlord doesn't.)

I took a shower, rinsed out the dye, and pampered myself with some scented powder before slipping into my favorite jeans and a gray T-shirt with Shakespeare's face on it. I flopped into my papasan chair and considered the reading material on the steamer trunk that was my coffee table. My brother had lent me a biography of Howard Hughes; I had a Nora Roberts book from the library. Not in the mood, I decided. My life needed a little mystery. I opted for an Agatha Christie off the shelf above me. Eventually, three chapters into *What Mrs. McGillicuddy Saw*, I wandered back into the bathroom to take a look at what I'd done.

I was expecting the worst. I'd burned myself on numerous occasions: the bad perms, the "no Novocain" decision, the jalapeño eaten on a dare, the downright loony choice of watching my cousin's colicky six-month-old for a weekend—I could go on. To my amazement, I liked what I saw in the bathroom mirror. Not only did I look perky as a blonde, I looked like I'd been born a blonde. I have green eyes and pale skin, and I'd serendipitously chosen a shade that accentuated them.

Jack had told me on more than one occasion that I was beautiful; my mother had told me that I had "good German bones." Now, for a moment, I thought I could see what they'd meant. I fancied that I looked like a sort of poor man's Elke Sommer. I pouted in front of the glass like a ferocious supermodel until I was quite sick of myself; then I decided to prowl around the building in hopes of a purposely accidental meeting with my brand-new ex, Jack.

I found him in the tiny laundry room, a small addition Mr. Altschul had built on the back of the ground floor of his large Victorian house (now a three-flat apartment accommodating the aforementioned German landlord, attractive ex-lover, and newly blonde me). Jack was stuffing all his clothes into the washer, darks and lights alike. He was obviously still angry about our fight, because he was jamming things in with extra force, as though his clothes offended him. I stepped casually into the room, ostensibly to check for an unused washing machine. Jack took one look at me, and his hands flew to his stomach and one knee came up as though I'd hurled a softball into his abdomen.

"What did you do to your hair?" he gasped.

"Isn't it obvious?" I asked, curling a blonde strand behind my ear.

"Are you nuts?"

"Is the washer available?"

"For God's sake, you couldn't just talk it out with me? You had to go and turn yourself into someone else?"

"I like it. Don't you like it?" I think my tone made clear that I wouldn't be happy with anything but an affirmative response.

"Madeline—"

"What?"

We faced each other, our unresolved argument still sitting like an iceberg between us. Since the crux of it was Jack's tendency to control me, his protest against my hair-color choice was not, I thought, the wisest response.

He finished shoving his clothes into the washer, hastily sprinkled some Tide over them, shut the lid, and cranked the knob with energy. I had always admired Jack's athleticism, being rather sedentary myself; even now I could appreciate his well-shaped, tanned forearms as they strong-armed the coin slot. He turned to face me, trying to keep his emotions in check.

"Okay, I don't know what you want, Maddy, but I don't think *you* do, either."

"You've decided that for me?"

"Stop it."

"Are you going to acknowledge that I'm an adult woman who can make her own decisions?"

"I never doubted it." He folded his arms defensively in front of his chest. He was wearing a solid black T-shirt and some old gray jogging shorts. I felt a pang of sadness, because I used to borrow the outfit.

"You opened my mail, Jack."

"It was a second notice—"

"It was *my* second notice!" I heard my voice shrilling and I toned it down. "If I got a hundred notices, it wouldn't change the fact that they were addressed to me!"

Jack ran a hand through his wavy brown hair. He looked around the laundry room as though hunting for inspiration among the detergent and clothespins. I felt for him. In the year we'd been together, arguments had been rare, and always resolved. This one, to his surprise, wasn't going away.

Jack sighed and shrugged. "I'm sorry I made you angry. But I've got to tell you, Maddy, if I thought I was doing something wrong, I wouldn't have done it. I mean, if you don't know me by now . . ." He let the sentence hang there. We faced each other like duelists.

"I guess I feel married to you," he continued. "I don't think it's a big deal for a husband to open his wife's mail. I feel like a husband. We love each other, we sleep together, we're monogamous, we practically live together—"

"In separate apartments."

"Only because you want it that way. So we both have some control here, don't we, Madeline?"

I took a deep breath and made myself unclench my fists. "I've got to be up early tomorrow to do some work, so I'm going to bed now. I suggest you steer clear of me unless you are willing to address the actual issue. This isn't about love or marriage or which bed I choose to sleep in. This is about acknowledging my autonomy and my rights, just as you would for a male best friend who was your roommate."

His jaw dropped. "Are you calling me sexist?"

"If the narrow shoe fits," I yelled over my shoulder as I stomped out of the room.

I caught a glimpse of Mr. Altschul's nose as he pulled it back into his apartment, and felt a blush of shame. We had turned this into *One Life to Live* in a matter of hours. I doubted our landlord would request our departure, since he was obviously thrilled by the fireworks, but I felt shame nonetheless. Aside from my aforementioned erratic moments, which were relatively rare, I was a reasonable, even reserved person. My brothers, Fritz and Gerhard, called this trait "the Too-Teutonic Reserve," since they saw it as a hereditary flaw passed down by my German-immigrant parents—one that prevented meine Bruder from bonding with numerous women. My brothers liked Jack very much. They weren't going to be thrilled by my news of a breakup, especially since they think everything I do is irrational. They think I chose to date Jack, a rare family-sanctioned decision, because they were there when we met and they helped to influence the outcome—about which they are, of course, wrong.

It was the guitar that made me fall in love with him. He'd been play-ing it on the day I moved in. (My mother had won me the apartment by chatting with Mr. Altschul in German.) I was sitting, exhausted, on top of a packing box and eating ice cream with my sweaty siblings, who had hauled in all of the heavy stuff. Suddenly, a melody wafted through the window, unmistakably played on a guitar and pretty certainly coming from the apartment above. Then a voice began singing, as though my own troubadour had come to woo me at my window. I wondered vaguely if the singer was a professional.

"What's that?" asked Fritz, two years my junior, distracted for a moment from his double-scoop cone, his foxlike face alert, his red mustache dripping.

"A guitar, Brain," answered Gerhard, two years my elder, still study-ing his ice-cream sandwich's label, his dark brows furrowed above his handsome face.

"The song, I mean." Fritz shoved what remained of his cone into his mouth and then, in an awesome feat, continued to speak: "The awhtist."

"Gordon Lightfoot," I ventured. He was playing "That's What You Get for Lovin' Me."

"It's acoustic," Fritz sneered.

228

"That's right. We forgot you don't like instruments that can't be plugged in," Gerhard quipped.

"Or musicians who play more than one chord progression over and over," I added spitefully, referring to Fritz's garage band, the Grinning Bishops, who had once practiced in my parents' garage but had mercifully moved their act to his friend Chuck's basement. Apparently, things were different now, though, because Fritz actually made more money some weeks with the band than he did working as a manager at Barnes and Noble. In any case, our family tended to remember those appalling years, with discordant notes and loud feedback still echoing in our nightmares.

Some kids grow out of that nasty argumentative phase, but my brothers and I still argue—I think, sometimes, it's to express our closeness. We feel we have the right to be sarcastic because we're family. We don't strike each other or fling things, but we have potentially cruel tongues.

Still, it was my brothers now whom I went upstairs and called. They share an apartment, so they were able to yell at me on two extensions.

"Wait until Mom hears this," Fritz threatened. "She's gonna have a nutty. She was crocheting some sort of little bag for your wedding."

"Shut up, Fritz, that's a secret," boomed Gerhard in my ear.

"Well, it doesn't matter now, does it? She dumped him." The two of them began an argument of their own, and it comforted me briefly, until I heard Jack playing his guitar upstairs. He knew I could hear him; I'd confided that to him long ago. I could even hear lyrics when my window was open, which it was now. Jack was playing "Devil Woman." Real subtle.

"We weren't even engaged," I protested.

"It doesn't matter, Madman," Fritz said. "He's the one she wants you to marry. Everyone does. He's not a total loser, like some we could name, so of course you had to break up with him." Fritz, as usual, opted for criticism over compassion.

Gerhard was gentler, by a hair. "Really, Madman, we did like him. I have to wonder if the problem isn't just something you're manufacturing, maybe for a little drama?"

"Okay, I'm hanging up now," I yelled just before I slammed down the receiver.

I rubbed at my eyes. There was no one who was going to be on my side here, except maybe good ol' Gloria Steinem, and I didn't think she'd be returning my e-mails, or voice mails, or whatever kind of mails I might send her.

This was where Fate intervened. Jack had switched to something more melancholy; it sounded like some sort of sea chantey. I imagine he thought it would send me running up there in a diaphanous gown, seeking a night of passion in his bed. In his defense, I suppose it had happened before. I'm only human, and I do love the guitar. However, despite the sound of the lonely sailor above me, I remained on my couch, and I was back into Agatha Christie and *Mrs. McGillicuddy* when the phone rang. It was Fritz. He'd forgotten to tell me, in his anger, that Logan Lanford had disappeared. Naturally, Fritz was holding me personally responsible.

ABOUT THE AUTHOR

Julia Buckley has taught high school English for seventeen years, is married with two sons, and lives in the Chicago area. This is her first novel. Find out more at www.juliabuckley.com.